# MISTER BLACK

## IN THE SHADOWS - BOOK 1

## P. T. MICHELLE

LIMITLESS INK PRESS

MISTER BLACK

IN THE SHADOWS - BOOK 1


## In the Shadows Series
## Reading Order

*Note: Mister Black is the only novella. All the other books
are novel length.*

**DEAR READERS**: The **In the Shadows** series must

be read in the following order, books 1-3: **MISTER BLACK, SCARLETT RED**, and **BLACKEST RED.** The first three books tell Sebastian and Talia's happy-ever-after story. Cass and Calder's epic love story follows in books 4-5 with **GOLD SHIMMER** and **STEEL RUSH**. Be sure to read books 4-5, since you'll also get to visit with Sebastian and Talia as they play key roles in Cass and Calder's story before you dive into books 6 and 7, **BLACK PLATINUM** and **REDDEST BLACK**, which are stand alone Sebastian and Talia passionate adventure stories. Then I swing back to a new Cass and Calder stand alone story , **BLOOD ROSE,** coming in June 2018. You've got lots of great reading ahead of you!

*Whatever your passion, never, ever give up!*

# COPYRIGHT

Mister Black - Copyright 2014 by P.T. Michelle

Print ISBN-13: 9781939672223
Print ISBN-10: 1939672228

To stay informed when the next P.T. Michelle book will be released, join P.T. Michelle's free newsletter http://bit.ly/11tqAQN.

Cover credit: Cover designed by P.T. Michelle

V07122018

# SUMMARY

*When Talia crashes a masked party, the charismatic and dominant Mister Black is the one man who can either help or expose her. Neither can deny their attraction, but what happens when one hot night together turns into so much more...*

We all have someone who crossed our path and fundamentally changed us. That one person who blew through our lives, their presence forever stamped on our psyche. They linger in our thoughts, in our hearts, and in the decisions we make. A soul crusher or a dream maker, depending on the perspective.

My person is Mister Black.

I didn't know him by that name when I first met him.

I didn't know him at all, but the impression he left behind was just as powerful as the name I call him today.

He is Black: a deadly enforcer and masterful seducer.

I am Red: a justice bleeder and willing participant.

Together we are passion. Colors colliding through each other's lives.

When our secrets converge in a passionate encounter, stepping out of the shadows just might be worth the risk.

*DEAR READERS: The **In the Shadows** series must be read in the following order, books 1-3: **MISTER BLACK, SCARLETT RED**, and **BLACKEST RED**. The first three books tell Sebastian and Talia's happy-ever-after story. Cass and Calder's epic love story follows in books 4-5 with **GOLD SHIMMER** and **STEEL RUSH**. Be sure to read books 4-5, since you'll also get to visit with Sebastian and Talia as they play key roles in Cass and Calder's story before you dive into books 6 and 7, **BLACK PLATINUM** and **REDDEST BLACK**, which are stand alone Sebastian and Talia passionate adventure stories. Then I swing back to a new Cass and Calder stand alone story , **BLOOD ROSE,** coming in July 2018. You've got lots of great reading ahead of you!*

## IN THE SHADOWS Series reading order:

## BEFORE I LEARNED TO LOOK FOR RAINBOWS

## THE PAST

"*I* hate him. I hate him, I hate both of them." The words seethe from my mouth in a hiss as I barrel through the unforgiving, frigid downpour. Water sloshes inside my holey tennis shoes with each pounding slap against the trash-strewn sidewalk. I have no idea how far I've run. A couple miles? Ten? It feels like forever. A car drives past, its wheels splashing up a spray of water. I barely give it a glance. I breathe in short, rampant pants, my chest folding inward, crushing my heart. Images of little Amelia's chubby cheeks, pale blonde hair, and chocolate brown eyes flicker through my mind in a torturous, endless loop.

She was so very still. She's gone now. All because of innocence and curiosity.

No—because of spineless weakness and indifference.

I'll never hear her say "Talia" again or feel her sweet arms clutching me tight as I lift her into a hug. I choke up again.

Nausea churns in my belly.

I stumble as my thighs begin to shake.

Before my legs give out completely, I slow to a brisk walk-run and wrap my arms around my quaking body. The light from the car's taillights fades, while the cold rain mats the hair that has unraveled from my braid to the sides of my face. Welcoming the harsh pelting, I rip at the elastic on the end of my hair, then tear my fingers through the thick braid, yanking the long red locks free.

An hour ago, I'd rushed straight to my personal sanctuary like I always did when I needed to calm down or think. The fire escape outside my window couldn't soothe my shredded emotions this time, but it did give me an exit from my life. I couldn't climb down fast enough. And now I'm standing here in the freezing rain without a coat. Not a very smart move for someone who never plans to return.

When I see a man lying on a tattered couch butted against the curb up ahead, my insides tense. I glance around, trying to make sense of the neighborhood I've stumbled into. It's in the same rundown state as my neighborhood on the Lower East Side, but nothing looks familiar.

I straighten my spine and keep up my brisk pace. *Don't look at him. Don't let him see that you're afraid.* All I want to do is call my aunt, but I don't know what to say. How to begin? At this point she's already home from her shift. *Little Amelia. Oh, God.* I squeeze my eyes closed briefly and whimper. Aunt Vanessa could've done better than her stuck-in-a-rut boyfriend, since all Walt had going for him when they first met was steady work as a carpenter. But becoming Amelia's "mother"—whose real mother skipped out on Walt when Amelia was just four months old—seemed to help my aunt finally find some contentment. With Amelia in our lives, she'd been much more laidback and less intense.

Somewhere in the distance a police siren goes off, making me jump. I immediately want to run, but force myself to stay calm and keep up my steady pace. I have no idea where I'm going. Just away from the siren.

As I pass the bum, even in the rain I smell his stench. I wrinkle my nose and hold my breath while I keep moving forward. Suddenly a hand grabs my shoulder, tugging me around.

"Hey, you got any change?"

While he stares at me, I throw my hands wide, partly to shrug off his hold, but also to look aggressive and confident as pent-up rage and anxiety spikes. "Do I look like I have any change on me?" He might have a scraggly beard and need a bath, but he's the one wearing a freaking coat and knit cap, while I'm in skinny jeans and a thin sweat-shirt in a forty-degree downpour.

His watery green eyes slide to the thin gold chain with two floating heart charms around my neck. "You could give me that."

"Yeah, right." When I turn to walk away, he grabs my arm.

"Come on, kid. I know you could get another one."

"Let go of me!" I try to sound tough, tugging hard against the man's tight hold.

When he starts to reach for the delicate chain, I wrench out of his grasp and take off in the direction I'd come from. He'll have to rip it off me. My aunt worked two jobs to buy me the necklace for my eleventh birth-day. She gave it to me two years ago, not long after we moved in with Walt and Amelia. "The second charm is for Amelia," she'd said. "When she's old enough, I'll buy her a necklace and you can give her one of the hearts. Then, the two girls in my life will have a matching pair."

Ill-fitted boots *clomp,clomp* on the pavement not far behind me, knotting my stomach. He's surprisingly fast for a guy who loafs around all day. Just when he catches up to me, someone calls out in a strong voice, "Leave her alone, Harry." We both stop on the sidewalk.

The rain slows to a lighter shower as the guy chasing me swivels around. He snorts at the older teen, who's staring at him across the roof of an idling black Beamer.

"Well lookee who's come a slummin'. It's been a while, Blackie." He lifts his bearded chin toward the car. "Why don't you give me some money instead?"

The guy snorts and slams his car door, then comes around the front of the car. "So you can go buy some liquor with it? I don't think so." He fishes his hand in his front jean pocket, pulls out a receipt and hands it to the guy. "Take this up to Jake's Diner. I've paid for you to have ten meals. If you hurry, you can grab your first one tonight before they close."

Harry grunts, then snatches the receipt, tucking it in his pocket. He doesn't even look twice at me as he passes, apparently taking the guy up on his offer without so much as a thank you.

Once the homeless man turns up another street, the guy looks at me. "I've never seen you around here before. Did you just move into the neighborhood or something?"

While the drizzle plasters his black bangs to his scalp and makes the ends of his hair brush his coat collar, I skim my gaze past his shadowed face to his fancy car, then back to his nice leather jacket. He doesn't belong here. "I don't live in this neighborhood," I say.

"Where do you live? You shouldn't be out here alone." He pushes his hands in his pockets and looks up as the rain finally stops, his breath pluming in the crisp air. "Can I give you a ride somewhere?"

His gaze returns to me as he steps into the lone lamppost's light. He's nice looking with sharp cheekbones, but his eyes snag my attention. They're so unusual, I'm mesmerized; one is dark brown and the other is a striking brilliant blue. He edges a bit closer.

Wary, I take a step back and quickly look down at my hands. Red stains every crease and crevice, caking my knuckles and along the lifelines in my palms. A moment of panic sets in that he'll see it. I curl my fingers inward, blinking rapidly, then glance down once more. My hands are clean. It must've washed away in the downpour.

Wishing I could pop my skull open for an equally thorough cleanse, I clench my jaw to stop my teeth from chattering. Now that I'm no longer running and amped up on pure adrenaline, the cold is creeping over my body. "You—you're not from this side of town."

He glances over his shoulder toward the street he'd driven to earlier and says in a low tone, "I used to be." Facing me, he shrugs out of his coat. "It'll always be a part of me."

Before I can move, he steps forward and drops it around my shoulders. "Here, I can tell you're freezing."

Instant warmth and the smell of rich leather envelop me. I can't resist pulling the coat tighter. "Thanks," I mumble, hiding my face behind my wet hair.

My guess is he's around seventeen or so, but he's much taller than most boys his age. I feel like a dwarf beside him.

"Where do you live?" he asks while lifting a strand of my hair over my shoulder so he can see my face.

I glance around, anxious realization cramping my stomach. Where *am* I going to sleep tonight? How will I eat? What I wouldn't give to have the security of ten meals in my pocket right now. "I don't know," I whisper.

Concern creases his brow. "You don't know where you live?"

I shake my head and look away, afraid he'll see too much in my eyes. "I can't go back."

"Do you have someone who loves you at home? Some family?"

My gaze shifts to his steady one. "Yeah."

"Then that's all that matters." He turns and walks to his car, opening the passenger door. "Come on. I'll take you home."

I shake my head in fast jerks. "I can't."

He steps toward me, his voice suddenly tight. "Has someone hurt you?"

Clamping my mouth shut, I bow my head. "I've done something horrible."

Wet, cold fingers touch my chin, but I pull away, tension building inside.

"No matter what you've done, family forgives," he says softly. "It's like the tide every morning and evening, sunrise and sunset, and a rainbow after the rain stops and the sun shines."

A raw edge of hope laces his comment—as if he needs to believe in his own words. Instead of putting me off, it fuels my courage purely because he used to live here. He knows it's not easy. I glance up, then frown, worried. "Rainbows don't always come out."

He smiles broadly, a dimple appearing on his right cheek. "The brilliant colors are always there. You just have to know where to look."

The confidence in his answer gives me courage. I follow him to his car, then quickly slide into the passenger seat.

As soon as he settles behind the steering wheel, I ask, "Do you have a towel or a blanket? I'm dripping all over your leather seat."

He takes in the water pooling under my butt, dripping off my jeans onto the supple black leather. Smirking, he starts the engine. "I know."

"This isn't your car, is it?"

The look he gives me is both defiant and amused. "Nope."

*Oh God, am I in a stolen BMW?* I start to reach for the door handle when he presses on the gas and the car zooms forward.

"I didn't steal it. I'm just borrowing it."

*Uh huh. And I didn't just commit a crime. Two liars sitting side-by-side.*

"Where do you want me to take you?" he asks while I chew the tip of my thumb in indecision. The last thing I need is to draw police attention. If we get stopped, I'm not confident my black sweatshirt will hold up under the indoor lighting at the police station. Does blood glow under florescent lights? Or is that black light? I wrack my brain trying to remember from TV shows. Either way, I don't want to find out. "I should just probably walk."

He turns right onto a main road. "Or I can just drive for a while if you want."

The car smells like leather and "new car" scent, and its warmth feels so good. For a second I consider trying to fall asleep. Maybe then I'll wake up to discover all of this has been one big nightmare. I shrug off the fantasy. The last thing I want is to get out and have to walk around in the cold night air with sopping wet clothes, so I nod.

We drive for about twenty minutes when he finally breaks the silence. "What's your name?"

I shake my head.

"You want to talk about it?"

I bite the inside of my cheek and stay quiet.

Sighing, he pinches the top of his nose, then rubs his thumb along the curve of his eyebrow. "I used to live in that neighborhood back there, remember?" he says softly.

Something about the sympathy in his voice cracks through, creating a knot in my throat. Suddenly I'm overwhelmed with emotion. No matter how I try to justify my actions, I'm a terrible person. Panic sets in and I start to breathe hard. Clutching my chest, I pant out, "Stop the car. Just stop. I can walk. I need to go."

He quickly maneuvers through traffic and pulls off to a side road. I bend over and wheeze, trying to catch my breath.

A warm hand kneads my shoulder. "It's okay. Breathe. Just breathe."

"I. *Can't*," I choke out, fingers clawing at my throat. It's closing up. I'm smothering.

He pulls my hand from my throat and gently cups the back of my head. "Hey, I'll breathe with you, okay? Take deep breaths. Like this. Through your nose, then out of your mouth. In and out. In and out."

As he rubs his thumb along my wrist, I take a breath and follow his lead, trying to slow my racing heart.

Several seconds pass with us just breathing quietly.

"That's it, Red." He gives an encouraging smile. "You'll be okay."

Usually I would totally hate being called Red—second only to Freckles—but right now his teasing in the middle of my dark, spiraling reality is so crazy and absurd, it's exactly what I need.

Once I'm breathing normally, I pull away from his hold and press my shoulder into the door. "I'm fine," I say in a low voice.

He leans back against his seat, resting an arm on the steering wheel. "You get those attacks often?"

I start to shake my head when my gaze zeros on the watch he's wearing. I don't know the brand, but by the look, it's probably worth more than a year's salary to most people in my neighborhood. I nod to his watch, eyebrow hiked. "You're from around here, huh?"

He follows my line of sight, then raises his arm to look at the watch. Taking it off, he holds it out to me. "Here, take it. I don't want it. The price I paid for it was too high."

The pain in his voice is real, as real as the one raging inside me. "What happened?"

He sets the watch down on the seat between us, his gaze locked on the clock face. "I lost my mom."

"I'm sorry," I murmur.

Glancing up at me, his unusual eyes hold heartfelt sincerity. "You'll never know how much family means until they're gone. I didn't have a choice, but you do."

I wish I'd known my mom. She committed suicide when I was a baby. My dad was never in the picture, apparently. I didn't have a choice either, but I stay silent.

He gently tucks a wet strand of hair behind my ear. "Don't run away. Go back and tell them you love them. Whatever you've done, they'll eventually forgive."

My body stops shaking while he talks. What he says makes sense, but all I can do is hope "family bonds" will be enough. Thinking about it churns my stomach, so I tilt my head and focus on him. "Why did that guy call you Blackie?"

Amusement glittering in his gaze, he shuts his blue eye and stares at me with his brown one. "Because of this. He says the dark one makes me Black Irish."

"Why *do* you have different colored eyes?"

"It's not entirely unheard of."

I shake my head at his offended tone. "I've seen a person with one green and one blue eye, and another with a hazel and a green eye, but never eyes like yours. They're—"

"—Odd, disturbing, distracting. Let me guess...you don't know which one to focus on, right?" he supplies, a smartass smile on his face. "I've heard it all before."

I smirk. "I was going to say, 'Like night and day. They're unique.'"

"Most people don't ask about my eyes so quickly. They usually dance around it a bit first."

"Oh, sorry," I say, wincing.

"Don't be. Thanks for making me feel a little less like a freak of nature." He puts the car in Drive, then pulls back onto the road. "Ready to tell me where you live now?"

There's no way I'll let him drop me off in my neighborhood, so I give him the name of a street a few blocks over from mine. Fifteen minutes later, he pulls outside an apartment complex and gives the neglected building a once over. "Is this you?"

I nod and reach for the door handle.

"You okay now, kid?"

"Why are you calling me kid? You're not that much older than me."

His brow puckers. "You can't be more than what, fourteen?"

*Like age gives you a free pass from bad shit.* I don't want his pity. Rolling my eyes, I force a light tone. "I'm old enough not to share that with you."

"Hey," he calls as I quickly slide out of the seat and shut the door. The electric window zips down. "Take care, Red."

"You too, Blackie. Thanks for the ride."

Nodding at my quick comeback, his lips quirk upward. He closes the window, but doesn't drive away until I climb the stairs and reach for the button panel to unlock the main door. Of course, I don't know the code, so I just pretend and punch in random numbers.

The second the Beamer rounds the corner, I take off. I'm halfway down the street before I realize I never gave him his jacket back. Grimacing at my forgetfulness, I pull the lapels closer together and soak up the coat's warmth, thankful for it.

When I get within a couple blocks of my neighborhood, my teeth won't stop chattering. My jeans feel like slabs of stinging ice pressing against my skin. Just when I stop and rub my hands against my thighs to help warm them, a strong smell of smoke wafts in the air. Discomfort forgotten, I take off running once more.

A massive crowd stands around my building watching the chaos. Fire truck lights are flashing and the firemen are doing what they can to extinguish a massive fire that's billowing out of the gaping hole on the fourth floor. People are talking, rumbling about an explosion. "Was it gas?" someone asks.

I cover my mouth to hold the scream inside. I can't let it out. My fingers tremble like a junkie going through withdrawals. Our apartment and the conjoined apartment next to it—where Walt spends most of his down time with his buddies, drinking and hanging when Aunt Vanessa isn't home—are both gone. With a blast like that, will there even be bodies left to bury? The thought makes me nauseous.

Finally the tears come. For Amelia. Not for Walt.

What caused it? Was it a gas leak in the other apartment? Oh God, was Aunt Vanessa in our apartment when it happened? She should've been there an hour ago.

*No. No. No. Please, no!* All the family I have left. Gone.

Just as my legs start to buckle, someone screams, "Talia!" I jerk my head around toward the voice. My aunt is frantically pushing her way through the crowd. When she's ten feet away, the people start to part and let her pass. As soon as she reaches me, her dark eyes roam over my face, anguish and relief in her expression. Tears streak her cheeks, but she's still wearing her work uniform and the bun in her dark hair is askew.

Guilt swells in my throat, making me croak when I try to talk. "I'm so sorry, Aunt Vanessa."

"You're okay. Thank God!" she says, grabbing me and pulling me into a tight hug.

"I need..." The words jam in my throat, wanting to be free. "I wa—want to tell you."

"Hush!" my aunt gusts in my ear. "The firemen won't let me go up, but I know..." she trails off, her voice cracking.

She's gripping me tight, tighter than she ever has before. As I hug her back, I realize that telling her the truth would be more painful for her than the one she's experiencing right now. Amelia might not have been hers, but she loved her like a daughter. Just like she has me, ever since my mom swallowed a bottle of pills when I was just a week old. Letting my aunt hold onto some pleasant memories is better than none, so I clamp my jaw shut and swallow my guilt and anger.

The wind picks up, encouraging the flames to spread.

Several more firemen burst through the crowd, and we have to move out of their way to let them pass. When my aunt and I turn to watch the men try to contain the blaze, our entire lives floating in the debris with the smoke, she says, "This is going to be hard for a while, Talia. It's just you and me now. Like it has always been."

"I know," I say and gulp back the anxiety clawing at my throat. We'll have to sleep in a shelter tonight and probably for a while until we figure things out. We have no other family. My aunt had only just finished nursing school and was in her first nursing job. Even with her salary, I know she depended on Walt's carpentry income —which was a crock. It's a good thing she'll never know the real truth—to make rent and her car payment. The idea of having to quit school and find a job gnaws at my gut. School's my only chance of going to college...of making a better life. Sighing heavily, I hunch my shoulders and slide my hands in my pockets to stave off the wind's sharp bite.

My knuckles drag against something metal, and I frown, curling my fingers around the object in the coat. When my thumb rubs across the watch's face, I realize he must've slipped it into the pocket right before I got out of his car. Sneaky car thief.

My grief for Amelia still heavy on my mind, I lean into my aunt's solid frame. She has always been much stronger than me.

When she squeezes me and says quietly, "We're all we have to depend on," I know we'll be okay.

One day.

I clutch the watch in my hand, fisting my fingers tight around the metal. That's not all we have to get us through. *Thank you for the rainbow, Blackie.*

# CHAPTER ONE

## EIGHT YEARS LATER

"**G**et up, sleepyhead," Cassie says before landing a stinging whack on my butt.

"Ow!" I jerk my head up, morning sunlight making me squint as I glare at her through the tangled red curtain of my bedhead hair. "What's wrong with you? The sun's barely up. I'm not going to the beach this early. It's probably too cold anyway."

Cassie's silky black hair slides forward over her shoulder as she giggles and rips the covers off me completely. "I know the Blakes are the real reason you came to the Hamptons with me for Spring Break. You should be thanking me. I'm about to make your wishes come true."

Her mention of the Blakes grabs my full attention.

Rubbing the chill bumps off my arms, I quickly sit up. "How'd you know?"

Cassie flops onto the bed beside me. "I'm your best friend." Sweeping her hand around her lavish bedroom and then toward the French doors that lead out to the beach beyond, she continues, "I know lazing around here with me isn't how you'd normally spend your Spring Break."

I shake my head and snort. She knows me so well. Since Aunt Vanessa's off on her umpteenth cruise with her new husband, I didn't have to go home and work a retail job for extra cash like I always have in the past. But just because my aunt married well this past year doesn't mean I'm going to stop working hard. It just gives me more time to work on my career, well...future career. The school newspaper is my "job" now, even if I'm not paid. "Okay, guilty, but how'd you know about the Blakes?"

She purses her lips and stares at her nails. "'Cause I followed you the other day."

My back goes ramrod straight. Forcing myself to relax, I hug the pillow, guilt knotting my stomach. "I really did want to spend some time with you, Cass. It's just that...well, I couldn't let this opportunity pass me by. Getting the real scoop on what happened with Mina Blake could be the story that helps land me my dream job at the Tribune when I graduate in May." Grimacing, I shrug. "Not that going to the Blakes that day did me any good. I couldn't get past her father to see Mina. I tried again yesterday at a restaurant in town, but her two older brothers are just as bad. They didn't let me within twenty feet of her. They're protecting her like hawks."

Cass's light brown eyes flash back to mine. "Maybe her roommate committing suicide really is why Mina withdrew from school. Her family's probably just being protective, Talia."

"No, there's something more to it. I know there is. Too many rumors are flying around campus. Stories that Bliss might be involved, something about a distribution ring."

"Bliss?"

I nod. "An upgraded form of Ecstasy and very expensive. Mina might know more. I want to hear what happened from her. If any part about the drug stuff is true, it just doesn't make sense to me that either girl would take part in dealing drugs. They both come from wealthy families; neither girl needed the money."

"Maybe they were taking the drugs too," Cass says.

"I didn't hear any rumors about drug use." *Just running drugs. But what made them do it? There has to be more to it.* The memory of Walt's stale beer breath, as he grabs my backpack and shoves a brown lunch bag inside it, comes back to me full force.

"Give these supplies to a carpenter buddy of mine on

your way to school, Talia. He'll be waiting for you over at the park gates."

"But I don't walk that way."

"You do today," he snaps. "And any other day I ask you to."

"But I'll be late for school."

"Then leave earlier. Who do you think pays for your aunt to go to nursing school? So shut your damned mouth and get going."

A scruffy guy in a ball cap tugs on his bill with stained fingers, then pushes off the fence when I approach.

"You got it, kid?" he rasps, snatching the bag I'd pulled out of my backpack to hand to him.

With dark stains under his fingernails, he looks more like a mechanic than a carpenter. My gaze stays locked on the H and F stamp on his hand as he digs through the bag. I recognize it as the Hounds and Foxes nightclub emblem, except the ampersand between the H and F is flipped in the wrong direction. *Why would the nightclub use a stamp with a backward ampersand? Do they not know it's backward?*

"What the fuck are you looking at?" he snarls.

"Nothing." I shrug and walk away.

Guilt flushes my cheeks that I'd played a part in dealing drugs all those years ago. I figured out it wasn't carpenter supplies a couple months later when I finally worked up the nerve to look in the bag one day after I left the house. Blue, pink, and white pills filled hundreds of plastic bags inside. It explained a lot about Walt's drinking buddies and their "man cave". The bastard and his cronies put together bags of Ecstasy for distribution.

I tried to confront Walt about it, because I was pretty sure Aunt Vanessa didn't know. She'd never put me at risk like that. The only good that came out of that conversation was that Walt promised me if I kept my mouth shut and did as he asked, he'd keep Hayes away from me. What else could I do? Aunt Vanessa hadn't finished her nursing classes, and I couldn't imagine leaving Amelia, so I studied in school, kept my head down, and delivered stupid bags.

"You okay? You look flushed?" Cass asks, bringing me back to the present.

I nod. "I'm just thinking about all the possibilities."

"Well, there might not be a reason for them dealing drugs." Cass shrugs. "Ultra rich kids do dumb things all the time. Sometimes just for kicks. Trust me. I've seen it all. It's like they live in a whole other world with a completely different set of rules."

I roll my eyes. "You're one of them."

"No, I'm *not*," she huffs. "Remember my dad's business didn't take off until I was a junior in high school. I wasn't born into wealth."

"Sorry," I mumble, feeling bad for judging. "It's just

that this whole 'not worrying about money' thing is a foreign concept to me."

She sighs and tilts her head. "You're attending one of the most prestigious colleges in the country and you still feel that way?"

"I got into Columbia on academics, not a trust fund, Cass."

"But you can *stay there* on your step-uncle's dime now, regardless of your grades. I guess what I'm trying to say is...it's time to relax a little. Your aunt is enjoying her time and you should too. Give yourself a break. Stop running a-hundred-and-ten miles an hour. You'll burn out before you're twenty-five."

*I have to land a great job once I graduate. I never want to be in the position my aunt was, depending on someone to take care of her. Being financially secure while seeking the truth and uncovering injustices will be the ultimate career for me.* "Wait? If you want me to relax, why are you going to help me with the Blakes?"

Her eyes sparkle with wickedness. "Because I have my own score to settle, and an exclusive masked party at the Blakes' house this upcoming weekend is the perfect opportunity to exact my revenge."

I raise an eyebrow. Who knew my friend had a vengeful streak? "I had no idea you knew that family. I would've just asked you to make introductions for me."

Cass touches her collarbone. "Oh, I don't know the Blakes. Celeste Carver does."

"Um, if you don't know them, how are we getting into this party?"

"All last week Celeste has been crowing on social media about how she's been invited to this exclusive event at the Blakes' estate this weekend." Picking up her phone, Cass scrolls to Celeste's latest post. "This morning she was bemoaning the fact she won't be able to attend."

"What does this Celeste chick have to do with you? And how does that get us into the party?"

Cassie grins. "Two reasons. One, I can pass for Celeste's twin. A fact she made me hate up until I saw her post this morning. And two..." Frown lines smooth out with her wide smile. "When the invitation explicitly states: Anyone who removes their mask during the evening will be escorted out, it occurs to me that I've finally found a way to pay Celeste back for making me look like an idiot back in ninth grade."

"That's a long time to hold a grudge." I frown slightly. "What did she do to you?"

"She told me that Jake Hemming liked me, but he didn't know how to ask me out. And since Celeste and I were supposedly friends—we had a couple classes together—I believed her. I thought Jake was cute too, so I put on my big girl panties, screwed up my courage, and asked him if he'd like to go out to a movie that weekend."

I can tell by her pinched expression things didn't go as planned. "What happened?"

Tears glisten in her eyes, humiliation reflecting behind the mist. "Jake laughed in my face in front of everyone. Then, he looked me up and down and said, 'You might look like Celeste, but you're nowhere near her level. It's bad enough she turned me down for Friday's dance, but I don't *do* middle class substitutes. Go back to being a nobody and stop trying to pretend to be someone you're obviously not.'"

"What a shitty bastard." I twist my lips in anger. "Let me guess, Celeste is incredibly wealthy?"

Cassie nods, fat tears spilling down her cheeks. Brushing them away, she says, "I know I should just let it go, but I've never been so humiliated, Talia. What she did made me feel less than worthless for a very long time."

I lift my hands toward her. "But you don't feel that way anymore. You're the most confident girl I know. Your fearlessness is what drew me to you."

She releases an ironic half-laugh. "Well, I wasn't always like this. I had many therapy sessions and some growing up to do before I found my own way."

Leaning over, I hug her close and whisper, "I had no idea." Cass's story just goes to show that you never really know a person like you think you do, even someone you're close to. Then again, she doesn't know anything about my past either.

Cass squeezes me, then leans back to smile. "Something my therapist said has stuck with me: 'Our pasts define us, but we don't have to let them rule us.'"

I offer a wry smile and fiddle with the gold chain around my neck, sliding the two floating hearts between my fingers. Keeping a part of Amelia close reminds me how quickly life can change. "If your past isn't ruling you, why are we going to this party?"

Cass flicks her tongue against her front teeth. "Because I'm in the mood for a bit of fun mischief by doing something that snobby Celeste Carver would never be caught dead doing. And hey, maybe we can finally get you laid in the process. At least the pool of candidates will have great pedigrees."

I scowl at her, hating that she's made it her mission this past year to pop my virginal cherry. It's like she sees it as a crime that I might graduate with it still in tact. Well, the figurative one. Most likely my battery-operated-boyfriend (aka BOB) took care of the physical one. The truth is, I just haven't found the right person yet. So far, none of the frat guys Cass hangs out with have done anything for me. Nor has any other guy I've met in class given me a reason to go beyond a coffee date. No one has measured up to that guy who taught me to look for rainbows. He's the one I think about during my BOB fantasies. I don't need a friend-with-benefits. Not when I have memories and BOB.

Cass wags her finger at me, snagging my attention. Her gaze narrows. "If you don't try to get out there and give some guys a chance, Miss Too-Picky-For-Her-Own-Good, I'm going to throw BOB in the trash and force you to lower your standards."

I glare at her, mentally vowing to move my vibrator's current hiding place as soon as I get back to school. "This party is a clandestine, not a *candlelight,* mission. Give it a rest."

Hopping off her bed, she waves her hands as if clearing my frustration from the room. "Hurry up and get a shower. We have to go costume shopping."

My eyes widen. "Costumes? You didn't say anything about costumes."

"Oh, didn't I?" She presses her finger against her pursed lips, then winks. "You're going to have to come up with a fun fake name too. The invitation also mentions that no real names are to be used."

I snort. "I can see how this party will be great for me, since apparently the whole Blake family is aware of what I look like, but if everyone's going to be incognito, how will anyone know you're supposed to be Celeste?"

Cass barks out a laugh, then flips her hand arrogantly in front of her, adopting a pretentious tone. "You have no idea how over-the-top Celeste can be. She's larger than life and acts like she's a movie star wherever she goes. You, of course, will come as my favorite guest, and all the guys there will wonder what wealthy family you hail from."

I snicker at her Celeste imitation. I haven't even met this Celeste girl, but I'm sure Cass has her down to a T. That kind of snobbish personality definitely stands out. Rubbing my hands together, I slide off the bed. "The five day countdown starts now. Let's get Operation *Revenge* underway."

# CHAPTER TWO

"*S*top fidgeting with your hood," Cass snaps as we wait for the butler to open the front door at the Blake estate. "There's no way they'll recognize you. Even *I* think you went to extreme lengths dying your hair blonde. A wig would've sufficed."

I drop my hands to my sides, tucking them under the red cape's velvet folds. Exhaling slowly to calm my racing heart, I say in a low voice, "I can't help it. If I get caught again, I'm sure a restraining order will be in my near future."

Cass purses her lips as she adjusts her black and white French maid's skirt. "Maybe give up the idea of trying to talk to Mina tonight. That's one way to guarantee you won't get caught."

"I'm not the only one with an agenda, Miss Vixen-of-

Vengeance," I say, raising my eyebrow behind my black mask. "Care to call yours off?"

Cass makes sure the black choker around her neck is centered, then adjusts her own black mask. "Not a chance." Smirking at me, she flicks something in front of my face. "Just in case."

My cheeks flame at the foil wrapper between her fingers. I smack at her hand. "Put that away."

Cass laughs and then folds it under her fingers while ringing the bell.

"Classy," I say in a low tone to her sheer delight.

As the chimes ring throughout the house, barely heard over the upbeat dance music playing inside, I skim my gaze over her costume's short skirt that barely covers her ass and spiked black heels. Cass had spared no expense on our outfits, keeping them authentic but also very sexy.

I'm wearing a thigh-high peasant style, off-white shirtdress over fishnet stockings and tall, spiked-heeled black boots. A black leather corset cinched over the dress, not only outlines my curves, it also pushes my boobs up to distracting heights inside the dress's scooped neckline. My only requirement for my costume was that it had a place I could carry my phone and a small notepad and pen. Hence my red velvet, calf-length cloak with a hidden side pocket. Red Riding Hood suited my needs.

We'd come forty minutes late on purpose. That way

the party would be in full swing, which meant people would be less likely to pay attention to our entrance. Cass and I exchange a knowing glance as the butler pulls open the door. Of course we chose "costumes of lowly status" on purpose. We might've come with agendas and roles to play, but we definitely agreed that irony should play a part too.

The Blakes' "beach" house is a gorgeous, sprawling estate. From the Tuscan flooring to its sweeping dual stairwells flanking either side of the atrium style main room, it gives off an opulent Italian villa feel. Five sets of French doors line the farthest wall, allowing a full view of the stone terrace, lavish pool and a private beach beyond. If I weren't on a mission, I'd explore every inch of this glorious home, but instead I hold my breath as the youngest Blake son, Damien, walks straight up to Cass and grips her hand.

Spinning her around, the rapier at his trim waist swinging with his movements, he says, "Celeste, my love. You're going to be very distracting tonight." His brown eyes glitter mischievously behind a black mask that blends into his clean-cut dark brown hair.

"Ah, ah..." Cass faces him, tick-tocking her finger. "It's Naughty Maid Yvette," she corrects him in a sultry bedroom voice.

While I suppress a chuckle, Damien reacts to her husky tone like any virile twenty-three-year old. A confident smile crooks his lips. "Ah yes, Yvette, then. I'm so very happy your plans changed." Bending at his waist, he sweeps his short black cape and rapier back, his black boots shining. "Would you allow this fox the first dance?"

Fox? My lips twitch at his name and affected Spanish accent; the Spanish word for fox is zorro. The Blakes might be overbearingly protective, but they're also creatively clever. I'll give them that.

Cass bats her lashes behind her black mask, her ruby lips smiling broadly. "Ah, Z, how can I deny a wily hero such a simple request?"

Sweeping her hand toward me, Cass says, "I've brought a plus one. I figured you wouldn't mind. Fox, meet Scarlett."

I nearly choke at the name she gives me. We'd argued about my fake name all the way up the long, sweeping drive. I wanted to go by something simple like Ella, but she wouldn't hear of it. She told me she'd surprise me with something fitting for my costume. As I mumble, "Nice to meet you," to Damien, my gaze darts to his brother, Gavin, who's approaching us in a custom made suit. Gavin might only be a year older than his brother, but his hazel green eyes are far sharper behind his black mask. Are the pointed ears along the edges of his mask *wolf* ears? Oy, irony abounds tonight.

Of course, he has already zeroed in on me. I swallow a nervous gulp. This is *not* good.

Even though Gavin wasn't home that day Adam Blake refused to let me see his daughter, Gavin spotted me instantly when I walked into the restaurant where the siblings were having lunch the other day. Before Mina even noticed me, Gavin had quickly escorted me out with a cutting threat of filing a restraining order if he ever saw me again.

*Shit!* My palms tingle as his calculating gaze lingers on my face. My heart short-circuits, taking my breath right along with it. Is Cass trying to get me arrested?

Gavin has almost reached us, when someone to my right takes my hand and presses warm lips to my knuckles. "I think the two 'hoods' should dance together for solidarity's sake. What do you say, Scarlett?"

I turn to look at my rescuer, but can only see the outline of his angular jaw. His dark green hood is pulled much lower than mine, cloaking part of his face in shadows. He's dressed in light brown buckskin pants and a matching shirt. A bow is crossed over his chest, and a knife and bundle of thin rope are hooked to the soft leather belt around his trim waist. A quiver of arrows shows just over his shoulder.

I quickly glance at the oldest brother, who looks annoyed at—oh, he's ticked at the hooded guy, not me, thank God—and squeeze the fingers holding mine. "I'd love to."

The stranger has two inches on Gavin, which is

surprising. Gavin's at least six-two. The hooded guy has to be the tallest one here. In my high-heeled black boots, I just reach his nose.

Without so much as a glance Gavin's way, my rescuer pulls me over to the sunken area farther in the atrium where others are currently dancing to the latest pop song the DJ has queued up.

He doesn't release my hand once we reach a spot to dance. Instead, he spins me around, saying, "You looked like a deer facing down a hungry wolf back there."

My hood slides off my blonde hair as I make the full turn and end up facing him once more. Gavin's gaze hasn't left us; he's watching me with an intense stare, so I smile up at my dance partner and let him continue to hold my hand as we dance. "I'm fine. What can a Wall Street type do to me? Bore me to death with financial stats?"

He flashes a quick smile, revealing perfect white teeth. Apparently my response amuses him, so I tilt my head and keep up the solidarity ruse. "I've never seen you in this part of the woods before. Come here often?"

Spinning me once more to the upbeat tune, his smile fades. "I only show up when someone needs rescuing. I'm Robin."

"Robin? Hmmm." I take in his size. "You're more like an eagle, swooping in and stealing the prey away from the wolf."

"If we're going for metaphorical names, Miss Scarlett," He chuckles, sliding his thumb over mine, "I have more in common with a raven than the eagle."

"Why can't you be an eagle?" I ask, relieved that Gavin seems to have given up on watching me. He's talking to some people by the bar now.

"Ravens are black as sin, stealing through the night." His deep baritone draws my attention back to him just as he switches his dancing pace with the new song starting up.

His mouth twitches slightly, like he's amused by an inside joke. Comparing himself to a raven is so down-to-earth, I'm thrown off and a bit charmed. This guy's not at all what I expected from the entitled types surrounding us tonight.

"Stealing through the night? Ooh, mysterious. How about I call you, Mr. Black?" I give him his name for the evening with a bestowing nod. Still holding his hand, I take a step back and spin toward him.

The second I hit his chest, his hood bends toward me. Even though I can't see his eyes, his steady regard is palpable.

"I'm Mr. Black now?" he says, sounding intrigued. "I suppose I'll take the moniker as a counter to yours, Miss Scarlett."

His quick wit combined with his amazing smell is stirring all my senses. My new favorite scent is woodsy cologne and leather. I'm thoroughly fascinated. Inhaling deeply, I look up into his shadowed face, enjoying our banter. "Hmmm, black and red *are* strong, bold colors."

"On their own, yes, but when they're put together, they evoke a passionate response."

My stomach flutters, reacting to the lower tone of his voice. *Are we still talking about colors?* "Very astute of you to notice. Most guys don't make the connection between colors and emotion."

"I'm conditioned to notice everything, Miss Scarlett," he says in a confident tone. "There's something about you. You definitely stand out."

*What does he mean by that?* I can't see his eyes, but I feel them scrutinizing my face, studying it. His perusal feels too deep, probing even. Everything inside me tenses. "Conditioned?" I force a light, curious tone and immediately spin away once more. "What line of business are you in, Mr. Black?"

"Security." With a quick tug, I'm rolled back against his chest, trapped in the circle of his hold. His smile disappears, his tone serious. "For the record, ravens are just as predatory as wolves, maybe even more so for their cunning, stealthy ways."

Why does it feel like he's giving me a chance to get out before I do something I'll regret? I put my free hand on his arm, intending to step back. *There's no way he knows who I am. I'm just projecting my fear of getting caught. Get a grip, Talia.*

But when his muscles bunch under my fingers and his arm curls tighter around me, my ears begin to ring, alarm bells clanging in my head. "How interesting," I say on a croak. God, had I avoided the wolf, only to walk into a far more devious hunter's trap?

Holding my breath, I mentally walk through my entrance to the party. What made me stand out? Did I do something to give myself away? My hair is blonde and the black mask hides half my face. I don't have any distinctive moles anywhere or tattoos on my body, and my eyes are green, not an uncommon color. Do I have a "tell" I don't know about?

While my insides start to rev, preparing for flight, he turns me fully toward him, a pleased smile canting his lips. "I'm glad that doesn't scare you away."

*What doesn't scare me...ravens? Oh no, he's talking about him being in security. Wait? Is he coming on to me?* Once my brain reconciles the lowered huskiness in his comment as definite interest, the fear subsides and my pounding heart slows. I finally remember to breathe.

As I drag in a lungful of air, his intoxicating smell filters through, relaxing the tension inside me. *What cologne is he wearing? I want to bathe in it. I feel both revved and boneless at the same time.* "You rescued me from a wolf. Why would I be scared away?" I bat my eyelashes and play my doe eyes up, trying not to show just how rattled I am. "You don't usually play with your food before you eat it, do you?"

Strong arms pin me to his hard body. "Depends." He dips his head, and his voice drops to a sexy rumble next to my ear. "Is that an invitation?"

The warmth of his mouth against my ear elicits a jolt of sizzling awareness. I've been hit on with blunt directness from guys who've had several drinks, but this kind of intimate, seductive innuendo, in the middle of a smart, sexy verbal exchange, throws me off-kilter. Goose bumps scatter across every inch of exposed skin, and I'm momentarily stunned into silence. Damn this man is dangerously potent. I don't know whether to run or jump his bones. I've never reacted to a stranger like this before. Then again, I've never had a man seduce my mind and my body at the same time. The combination electrifies every nerve ending.

"Invitation?" I breathe out.

Threading his fingers in my hair, he traces his thumb along my ear, slowly following its curves. "I wonder... what *does* Scarlett taste like?"

My breathing halts as his mouth glides across my cheek, my pulse thrumming.

"Take a breath," he murmurs against my temple, "Better yet, let's breathe together."

The assuredness of his comment, that he assumes I'll

let him kiss me, sends a shiver of delight rushing across my flushed body, and against my better judgment, I allow him to tilt my face up.

My fingers curl against his chest and I wait. For a kiss from an enigmatic stranger I haven't fully seen, yet I still feel inexplicably, irresistibly drawn to. It's crazy and I can't even blame alcohol since I haven't had any.

Just as he lowers his mouth to mine, we're abruptly jostled by a group of overzealous dancers who've apparently had more than their share of drinks.

He's forced to yank me against him or we'll both fall, but the jarring jolt is enough to knock some sense into me. The music rushes in my ears and it hits me; the song isn't even a slow one, yet we'd tuned everyone out but us for a short time. I laugh at myself, at how caught up I'd gotten, and push against his chest. When his arms don't budge, I clear my throat and look anywhere but at him.

We're bumped again by a couple of guys goofing off, their antics breaking us apart. One of the guys grips my waist to steady me, calling out over the music, "Sorry!" Pausing, the guy—whose thick-chested body would've been more suited to a Frankenstein than his Dracula costume—glances down at me, then quickly twists me into a fast dip, murmuring in a suggestive tone against my neck, "Hmm, how 'bout I carry you off to my lair."

Before I can tell him to release me, we're both yanked upright. Black has a tight grip on his shoulder.

"Release her, Nick." His tone is quiet, deadly.

"Chill man, just getting into my role," Nick says in a laidback tone as he tries to shrug him off.

Black's hand doesn't move. "I'm going to ask you nicely once more. Take your hands off her."

Nick narrows his gaze for a second, then releases me, raising his hands. "See, no problem."

"Step outside to the terrace and sober up."

"What?" Nick attempts to wave Black off, but before he can argue further, Nick's suddenly on his knees in the middle of the crowd. "Ow, you dick! Let go of my shoulder."

"Did. I. Stutter?"

Black manages a menacing tone without raising his voice. I watch the exchange, impressed with how quickly he moves. And the sheer lethalness he projects.

He must dig his thumb deeper for emphasis, because Nick suddenly winces in pain, hissing out, "Fine. I'll go outside."

Black nods toward the French doors. "Head out. I'd better not see you in here for at least a half hour."

The second Nick walks outside, Black's eyes fill with satisfaction and he says in a low tone while placing his hand on the small of my back, "The bastard's lucky I'm in a generous mood tonight."

"Thanks," I say. "I think that vampire definitely had his share of alcohol for the evening." *That was generous?*

If Cass were telling me this story, I'd be inclined to think of Black as an arrogant Neanderthal, but witnessing his primal instinctiveness in action, I realize his job is more than just a career choice; it's an extension of him. He defused the situation quickly and efficiently. Like a professional.

*Shit, what would he do with me if he found out why I'm here?* Anxious, I use the song's fast pace as an excuse to edge back from him a bit while I glance around for Cass.

As soon as my line of sight locks on her dancing with a guy with light brown hair dressed in a formal white uniform, I'm fully brought back to the reason I'm here. She sure had ditched Damien fast. I wonder how Mr. Uniform fits into her "Celeste revenge" plan.

I realize Black is watching me, so I tilt my chin toward Cass and her dancing companion. "Who's the Navy guy?"

He clasps my waist once more and spins us around, only glancing in their direction once we've made a full circle. "You recognize his uniform as Navy?"

"Everyone knows formal white is Navy. Who is he?"

"Not everyone." He shakes his head, his lips tilting in bemusement. "That's Calder."

"I thought wearing a mask was a requirement to get into this exclusive bash. Why isn't he wearing one?"

He shrugs. "Cald's decision not to change the

uniform is respected."

"Oh, he's really in the Navy?"

With his nod, I realize exactly what Cass is doing. A girl like Celeste would never cozy up to a military guy. One in a costume, with millions in the bank, sure, but she'd consider a sailor on a government salary way beneath her social tier. I glance around, and sure enough, some people have started to notice. I frown, watching Cass and the guy interact as they dance. Completely oblivious to the snide looks and furtive comments being bandied about, the guy dips his head down to hear what Cass is saying. When he straightens and lets out a deep laugh, wrapping his arm around her waist to tug her close, my college roommate grins.

The second I see her turn and swipe two glasses of champagne off the tray of a waiter walking along the edge of the dance floor, I stop dancing, my worry radar going off. "Excuse me. I have to speak to my friend."

He clasps my hand before I can walk away. "Leave them," he says in a clipped tone.

"You don't understand—"

"He's going back on mission in forty-eight hours. Let him enjoy his last bit of down time."

When I try to shake off his hand, his mouth tightens in a stubborn line. "It might be a year or more before he comes back. Let it go."

I raise my eyebrow, but realize he's right. Cass can't

do too much damage to the guy's heart in one night. Let him have some laughter and fun in his life. He probably doesn't get much of that if he's always going off on missions. I stop trying to pull away and turn back to him. "What kind of missions does he do?"

He draws me close as a slow song starts up. "Stuff he can't discuss."

*Hmmm, mysterious. I hope you know what you're doing, Cass.* "It sounds like you know him pretty well. Is he a friend of yours?"

"More like a brother. We practically grew up together."

The intriguing Mr. Black has said just enough to make me want to know more about him. I tilt my head, feeling at a disadvantage, since I can only see the lower half of his face. "Is your hood your mask for the evening?"

"Curious?" A slight smirk curves his lips. "What if I'm scarred under here?"

*You'd still be sexy as hell.* "You afraid to show your true self?"

"Absofuckinglutely," he says without hesitation, his voice gruff as he slides his hands up my back, then slowly turns me to the soft music.

I let out a low laugh, appreciating his directness. "For all I know, you could be totally silver under there and twenty years my senior."

"Would that matter?" he says smoothly.

"Not at all, Mr. Black. I just don't want to do anything that might give someone of your *advanced* years a heart attack."

Expelling an arrogant chuckle, he hooks his arms at the base of my spine. "How do you know I won't do something to make *your* heart pound out of control?"

"Well, they do say that with age comes wisdom," I goad, really, really wanting that hood gone now.

His lips twitch. "Mastery in anything comes with doing, not age, Miss Scarlett."

My blood whooshes through my veins, making me tingle all over. His ability to switch from direct bluntness to innuendo is so freaking hot. He's definitely mastered that. "Really? And here I thought age and wisdom go hand-in-hand."

"Not always," he says, releasing me.

I hold my breath in eager anticipation as he moves to slide the hood off. When the green material lands on his shoulders, revealing hair even darker than Damien's, I grin my approval. It's so dark I can't tell where his black mask ends and his hair begins.

The second his eyes connect with mine, full of seductive promises, my heart jumps several beats. One single brown eye and one brilliant blue eye stare back at me behind his mask.

## CHAPTER THREE

*I*t *can't be him.* But all I can think about is the young guy who has haunted my dreams these past eight years. I shake my head, but the spots forming in my eyes only get bigger right before my knees give out.

He catches me, hauling me fully against him. "Are you okay?"

Blinking to stay conscious, I press my hands to his rock hard chest, my pulse whooshing in my ears. His youthful, pretty boy features have grown more rugged and angular. He has a scar on his chin that wasn't there before. Did he have a dimple when he smiled earlier? It's not like I can ask him to smile for me now. His hair's shorter and his shoulders are much broader. He's grown a good four inches. Is it him? Here, of all places? Or am I losing my mind?

"I—need to go to the bathroom," I say, extricating myself from his firm grip. Pivoting around, I bolt away and dodge left around a couple dressed as Morticia and Gomez, then veer right past a group of girls dressed as the Spice Girls. I pause when I finally realize I have no freaking clue where the bathroom is.

A strong hand clasps mine, and he tugs me through the costumed crowd, up the few steps, through the bar/living room, where others are hanging out on barstools and sofas, ice melting in their cocktails. The main room is packed, but the crowd starts to thin a little as he leads me to a door along a far wall.

"Here."

"Thanks." I pause when he leans back against the wall, arms crossed. "I'll be fine."

He shakes his head, his voice steady and calm despite the loud revelry around us. "I'll wait for you."

"Go back to the party. I'll be out soon."

"I'll wait."

"But you really don't have to."

He touches his mask, then locks a determined gaze on me, nodding toward the bathroom. "You entertain me, Scarlett. A beauty wrapped in intriguing layers. I'm not letting you out of my sight all evening."

*Layers? What does he mean by that?* I don't know what to say, so I just walk into the bathroom and shut the door. With the music muffled somewhat, I splash cold water on my heated cheeks and stare at my reflection in the mirror.

Of course, there are other dark-haired men out there in the world with one brown eye and one bright blue eye. It's possible he's not the guy from my past. But the age is about right. I start to nibble on the tip of my thumb, when the movement he'd done just before he gestured for me to head into the bathroom—pressing his thumb against his mask, right where his nose meets his brow—hits me. It's the same mannerism that guy had done that night when I wouldn't talk to him. That must be how he expresses frustration. Too many similarities to discount.

Oh God! It *has* to be him. No wonder I was drawn to him; I even named him Mr. *Black*. Blackie-Black. Sounds like a band name. I exhale a low, half-hysterical laugh, my brain short-circuiting as my shaking hands grip the sink. I stare in the mirror, trying to get control of myself. Okay, so it's him, but I don't look anything like the skinny redhead he helped all those years ago. He probably doesn't even remember me. I was a blip in his evening of prankster boredom.

I stare at my reflection. My nose is free of freckles now. I'm a couple inches taller, with a woman's curves instead of the boyish figure I had back then. And until the color grows out, I'm blonde, not the redhead from that night. I doubt he remembers anything from that evening, other than he helped a freaked out girl get home.

I'd lain awake so many nights as I grew older, hoping I'd run into Blackie again, dreamed about it even. I'd planned out what I would say and exactly how I would thank him for helping me. Then he'd shock me by pulling me close and telling me he'd never forgotten me.

Now that I'm faced with reality, I'm terrified. My dream guy was young and didn't ask probing questions. This *man* runs in completely different circles, and he doesn't miss a thing. With his profession, he'll ply me with questions, wanting every detail.

He has no idea the things I've done. And he never will. I stare at the closed door, my heart aching a little that he'll never know the positive impact he had on me.

With a heavy sigh of regret, I glance around and try to refocus. I can't let myself be distracted any longer from my purpose for coming here tonight. First, I need to figure out how to ditch my highly-perceptive dance partner. Then, I'll find Mina. When my gaze lands on the raised window next to the toilet, an escape plan forms.

I peer outside at the dark, heavy clouds that have rolled in with a storm about to break. Thankfully the bathroom sits right next to a covered terrace. Glancing over my shoulder, I quietly lift the window sash, then move the bathroom chair under the window so I can climb out. Turns out, that's not an easy task while wearing spike-heeled boots and a long cloak.

Somehow I manage to slowly inch my way out the window on my belly. All I have left to do is lower myself over the sill, then drop the last foot to reach the ground. As I maneuver, ready to lower myself down, my cloak snags on the chair. "You've got to be freaking kidding me," I mutter.

Just as I swat at the cloak to try and unhook the material, a knock sounds at the door. "You okay in there?"

"I'm good. Just need a minute," I call out, heart speeding up while I desperately yank to unhook my cloak. The chair tilts and starts to crash to the tile floor. I panic and swing the cloak around. Thankfully I catch the small chair on the material, which only manages to trap my cloak even more.

Hanging half inside the raised window sill, I hope and pray Nick stayed right next to the French doors, or he's getting one hell of a panty show with the wind whipping my short skirt up my back. Ever so slowly I tug the cloak and finally free it, leaving the small chair on its side.

Exhaling a sigh of relief, I lower myself down, then drop to the ground.

As soon as I turn the corner of the terrace, intending to find my way inside through one of the French doors, I see a huge black dog blocking Nick's way back into the house.

The dog tenses at my movements, darting his gaze to me. When Nick tries to side-step him, the massive animal snaps his attention back to Nick, curling his upper lip in a snarl. Sharp white teeth flash in the darkness as a low growl erupts from his throat.

Now I know why Black had smiled briefly once Nick walked outside. That guy has a devious streak.

"Nice, doggie," I say nervously.

The dog doesn't make a move toward me, but he's not letting Nick budge. When Nick raises his hand and says, "Go get Gavin or Damien to call this mongrel off," the dog aggressively snaps at the guy's pants. I panic, worried he'll connect, so I stomp my high heel on the stone, hoping to distract the dog. Instead, he just growls deeper at Nick. The second I open my mouth to yell at him to back off, thunder booms quickly followed by a flash of lightning.

The dog yelps and pins his ears back, then takes off running across the patio, apparently seeking a safe place to hide. Relieved, I don't say a word to Nick as I quickly follow him back inside the house.

While Nick immediately heads for the dance floor, I keep my gaze on the wall where the bathroom is located. I can't see Black's dark head because of the crowd, but just in case, I keep my head low while scanning to check on Cass. Finally I spot her still dancing with Mr. Uniform. She's laughing and drinking, having a great time. Her dance partner is a good-looking guy, and I'm sure the uniform only makes him hotter in her eyes. Makes me wonder if Cass has given up her mission for a general good time.

I certainly haven't. Swinging my gaze back through the room, I wonder how I'm supposed to spot Mina among the costumed guests. The answer hits me as I watch the bartender hand someone a drink. Bartenders always know everything.

Once I finally shoulder my way through the crowd hanging around the bar, the blond bartender smiles at me while twirling a metal cup across the flat of his palm. "Hello there, Sexy Red Riding Hood. What can I get you?"

I shake my head and smile. "I'm actually trying to find the youngest Blake. Have you seen Mina around?"

Without meaning to, he gives away her general location by glancing toward the cordoned off stairwell. "Haven't seen her, sorry. Would you like a drink?"

"No, thanks." Ducking my head, I squeeze my way back through the throng of people wanting more drinks, then steer toward the stairwell, all the while wondering how I'm going to climb the stairs without anyone seeing me.

A velvet rope blocks the bottom of the stairwell. A

sign is attached to the middle of the rope, boldly stating: Private quarters. Not for Guests. Upstairs is off limits.

I cast a gaze over my shoulder. No one is paying me any attention. And Gavin is currently dancing with *two* girls at once. No way he's looking over here. The thunder is rumbling now, louder with each boom. The partiers' excitement amps with each new thunderclap and lightning flash brightening the room.

When the lights flicker and then dim briefly and the crowd whoops their enthusiasm, I reach for the rope's hook on the banister's spindle. Everyone's watching the storm's fury unfold; this might be my only chance to get upstairs undetected.

The moment my hand lands on the rope, something slides up my right wrist and a deep voice grates harshly in my ear, "Where do you think you're going?"

# CHAPTER FOUR

*I* glance down at the rope Black has cinched around my wrist. Frowning at him, I try to yank free, but he's made some kind of rope handcuff, latching our wrists together. "Let's go," he snaps in a curt tone, tugging me along.

All I can do is stumble behind him as he pushes through a swinging door. The moment we enter the kitchen, the couple getting it on against a far wall near the double oven glance our way. "Out," he barks at them. The clean-cut "biker" guy lowers the girl with devil horns to the floor and they quickly readjust their clothes.

Once they exit another door on the far side of the kitchen, the muffled thump of music outside the door has nothing on the sound of my heart hammering against my chest. Black hasn't said anything to me yet, but he's standing so close it's unnerving.

I refuse to look up at him while I try to unhook the rope on my wrist. "Take this thing off me!"

"I don't think so." He slowly wraps the trailing end of the rope around his other hand, cinching it tighter around our joined wrists. "Since you bailed out of the bathroom window, I'll assume you're here for some reason *other* than a good time. You have thirty seconds to use that smooth-talking mouth of yours to convince me not to have you arrested for trespassing."

I meet his furious gaze and square my shoulders. "I'm here to see Mina Blake."

Surprise flickers in his eyes. Apparently that's the last thing he expected me to say. Did he think I was a thief?

His mouth tightens. "What do you want with Mina?"

Exhaling, I tell him the truth. "I'm trying to get her side of the story as to why she left school."

"She left. It's done." He shrugs. "Why do you care?"

"I work for the school paper."

Brackets of disapproval form around his mouth. "Mina's a story to you? You're a gossip reporter?"

The low growl in his voice, the utter disdain when he says "gossip reporter" tenses my stomach. He might as well have called me a "shit slinger." I hold my ground and shake my head. "Investigative. I solve mysteries with words. Some things just didn't add up to me. I want to hear her side of the story."

"There is no side. She left. End of story."

His tone is harsh, protective. No matter how irrational it is, a part of me can't help but feel a little jealous. How well does he know Mina? I jerk my chin up, meeting his hard stare. "If that's all there is to it, then why is everyone being so protective? Why isn't she down here partying? Why is she upstairs?"

"This party was for her—" he begins, then cuts himself off, jaw tensing.

That sounded personal, like he genuinely cares about Mina. I touch his arm, my gaze locking with his. "Look, all I want to do is to tell the truth. I'm not interested in smearing Mina's good name. I believe there's more going on. There are rumors."

"What rumors?" he asks, eyes narrowing.

"That she was involved somehow."

His face shutters. "She wasn't."

"Then let me tell the truth. Let me talk to her. This story means a lot to me for personal reasons, but if she refuses to tell me anything, I promise to let it go."

He glances at the ceiling as if considering. Finally, he shifts his gaze back to me. "I can get you five minutes." He begins to loosen the rope on my wrist.

When I start to smile my thanks, he halts his movements. "And then you're going to tell me how you know me."

I feel my eyes go wide. Keeping my tone even, I shift my gaze to our hands. "I don't know you."

Just as I slip my hand from the slackened loop, he clasps my freed wrist and slides his thumb along the soft skin, tracing my veins. "Yes, you do. The first time our eyes met, I saw recognition in yours."

I lift my eyes to his and really stare, hoping to throw him off his assumption. "Your eyes are arresting, that's all."

His gaze darkens. "Nice try. I can tell the difference between surprise and recognition. Somehow you know me."

"I probably saw you in a picture with the Blakes," I say nonchalantly, shrugging.

For some reason my comment makes him laugh. "You know me, yet you *don't* know me. This is more intriguing by the minute."

I snort. "I assure you, Mr. Black, all I know about you is that you have a talent with knotted rope."

"You have no idea," he says cryptically, shooting a dark, suggestive look my way as he steers me to a door tucked into the back corner of the kitchen. "I look forward to getting to know you, Miss Scarlett. One hood to another."

We take a back staircase upstairs and pass through a

door, where he leads me down a long hall toward another door at the end. Knocking lightly, he waits until a feminine voice calls out, "Come in," then he says to me, "Wait here," before disappearing inside.

The door is solid wood, so I can't hear what's being said. Just that the girl raises her voice in anger, and then his low rumble follows. *She's not happy. Maybe I won't get those five minutes after all.* When the knob starts to turn, I quickly step away from the door before he opens it.

"You've got your five minutes. If she chooses not to talk to you, you will abide by your word. Understood?"

He's so commanding and gruff, like a drill sergeant, I resist the smartass urge to click my heels and salute. Barely. "Got it."

I'm surprised when he ushers me inside, then closes the door behind me. I kind of expected him to stand guard in the room or something. As I stare at the girl with the long golden blonde hair sitting on the window seat watching the storm rage outside, I realize he must be pretty close to the family to convince her to talk to me, however briefly.

"You have four minutes and thirty seconds," the girl says on a heavy sigh without turning.

I can see by her profile she's just as beautiful and aloof as she is in pictures. She's a third year student, just a year behind me. Well, until she withdrew this semester.

I lift my chin and step forward. "Why did you really quit school, Mina? May I call you Mina?"

She turns gorgeous brown eyes my way, her gaze hesitant. "What's your name?"

"Scarlett." Approaching, I pull my notepad out of my cloak pocket and something falls on the floor.

*Cass!* I mentally scream, my face flaming. I retrieve the gold foil packet and shove it back into my pocket, mumbling about annoying friends.

When I glance up, the girl's nose is elevated and her face closes off. "Apparently Sebastian was wrong about you. I just lost my best friend. I'm not in the mood to become fodder for some trashy tabloid bimbo. You can leave now."

"My friend put that in there as a joke," I say in a low tone, trying not to take offense, but the girl's anger has already shifted back to a glassy I-really-don't-care-about-anything gaze. The sadness in her eyes pulls at something deep within me.

I slip the notepad and pen back in my cloak and untie the ribbon at my neck. Holding the cloak in my arms, I slide the mask off and offer an apologetic smile. "It's only fair if you know who's asking you questions. I'm Talia...and I understand loss more than you know."

The girl's hooded gaze turns curious. "Who did you lose?"

"I lost someone...who was like a sister to me...when I

was thirteen. Her name was Amelia." I haven't talked about Amelia's death to anyone. The words come out stuck together and raspy, like pages in an old photo album opened after years of deep storage. My aunt refuses to discuss that night. I suppose it's just as painful for her, so we never talk about it.

Tears glisten in Mina's eyes. "Does it get any easier?"

I sit beside her on the window seat and meet her pained gaze. "Missing her hurts a little less each year, but I have a hard time letting the guilt go."

"Were you responsible somehow?" Mina's eyes are wide, empathy in the dark depths.

I press my lips together. "No, but that doesn't stop me from feeling like I could've done something to prevent it."

Her shoulders slump slightly. "I know exactly how you feel."

"Drugs contributed to Amelia's death," I say, watching Mina's expression. When she starts to glance away, I continue, "So you and I have that in common as well."

She jerks her attention back to me, indignant. "Drugs didn't kill Samantha!"

"Then tell me what did, Mina. My gut tells me there's more to the story than what has officially been reported. Your roommate wasn't really dealing drugs, was she?"

Extreme guilt washes over Mina's expression before she presses her hands to her face, mumbling, "We didn't want to do it. God, it's all my fault she's gone, but I can't say a thing."

I pull her hands from her face, bending down to look in her eyes. "Why not?"

She looks down at our hands. "Because others might get hurt if I do."

Squeezing her hand, I say, "How many more people do you think might get hurt if you don't speak up to stop it?"

She shakes her head, her voice a whisper. "Too many others' lives could be ruined. The blackmail runs deep."

"Blackmail? Were you and your roommate somehow coerced into distributing drugs?"

A slow nod.

"And others were too?" I continue.

When she nods again, I bite the inside of my cheek, fury flashing. This is no longer a story, but a mission. "How about if the article is totally anonymous?"

Hope lights her face, then her gaze dims. "Your name will be on it. They'll trace you back to me as the source."

"The author of the article will be anonymous too."

She looks at me in confusion, her expression uncertain. "Why would you do that? I know how much a big scoop like this would mean to you. You're studying journalism, right?"

My professors saw my potential and gave me special permission to start taking graduate level journalism courses as an undergraduate senior. I nod. "And yes, this story would give me a lot of career options after I graduate, but I don't want to earn them that way," I say, while I unclasp my necklace. Once I slide one of the hearts off my chain, I re-clasp it around my neck, then hold the heart out to her. "Here."

She takes the tiny gold heart. "I don't understand. Why are you giving me this?"

I nod toward the charm. "I was supposed to give that to Amelia when she was old enough. I'm giving it to you so you'll know that I'll keep my promise."

Tears of relief trickle down her cheeks before she abruptly wraps her arms around my neck in a tight squeeze, whispering, "Thank you."

Wheezing to regain my breath, I pull back and smile. "Are you okay with me taking notes?"

Mina nods and brushes the tears away, then takes off her own gold chain to slide the charm onto it.

Pen and notepad in hand, my gaze snags on the heart hanging on her necklace. I try to take a breath but my lungs seize and my throat closes up.

Her fingers drift to the charm. "Are you sure, Talia? It's a wonderful gesture, but I trust you'll keep your word."

I swallow the lump and nod. "It looks perfect on you.

Amelia had your coloring. It's nice to see what it would've looked like on her."

Mina smiles then nods toward the door. "Sebastian must really respect you."

I pause in the middle of uncapping my pen. "Why do you say that?"

"Because he wouldn't have just brought anyone back here to see me. Everyone has tried so hard to shelter and protect me, but Sebastian—" She pauses and giggles. "He's such a rebel. I love that about him."

*But he just met me. He really has no reason to trust me other than my word.* I try not to let her obvious adoration of Sebastian get under my skin. Jealousy is a useless emotion. "Well, I promised him I'd be fair."

Her brown eyes sparkle. "I know you will be."

"I have one request, Mina. I won't disclose my source for this story, but I also don't want you to tell anyone my name. Ever."

Her brow furrows. "Wait...are you saying even Sebastian doesn't know who you are?"

I shake my head. "And I'd like to keep it that way."

"Wow." She blinks a couple of times, completely thrown. "I'm really glad you turned out to be a good person and not some psycho."

I chuckle. "You should trust Sebastian's instincts in the future. Promise?"

She crosses her fingers over her chest. "I won't tell. No matter what. Okay, what do you need to know?"

Brushing my hair over my shoulder, I hover my pen over the paper. "Tell me how it all happened."

With a small nod, she dips her head and takes a deep breath. "We thought we were just delivering some mail for our professor. He said we'd get extra credit for our efforts, so no big deal."

When her voice drops off, I glance up from my notepad. "Let me guess...not so much?"

She nods, her forehead pinching. "We had no idea what was in that mail. After we'd both helped him out a couple of times, that's when the blackmail started. He said more packages had to be delivered or he'd accuse us of cheating and we'd be expelled. And if we tried to rat him out, Professor Jacobson assured us that the way he'd set the delivery scenarios up—he never gave us the other packages directly after those initial deliveries we did for him—guaranteed that nothing would tie back to him. Everything would point to us as the drug dealers of Bliss. Us! Two girls from the Hamptons. If we got arrested, our families would flip out and probably disown us. Samantha..." She pauses, choking up even mentioning her roommate. "She just couldn't take it anymore."

They'd been so trusting, and their professor had used his position of power over them to create the perfect drug runners. So much innocence manipulated and abused. I grind my back teeth. Walt gave me specific instructions, so it had to be the same for her. "How did you know where to go and who to deliver the packages to?"

Mina nods. "The drop locations rotated. The packages just showed up in our school mailboxes with a note taped to it telling us where to go. We knew who to deliver the package to by the nightclub stamp on their hand. It's a replica of the stamp for the local Clangers and Bangers nightclub, except the ampersand symbol is backward between the C and B."

"Very clever," I mutter, even as I feel the blood drain from my face. *Shit!* The stupid hand stamp was a signal? What are the chances someone else is using that same concept?

Mina doesn't notice my disquiet as she continues to talk about how they brush elbows with the guy so he'll know the drop is coming. I stare at the heart on Mina's chain, knowing it has found its rightful place. That explosion may have gotten rid of Walt's packaging operation—*had a rival drug dealer tried to take out the competition, i.e. Walt, Jimmy and Hayes?*—but one of Walt's buddies hadn't been there that night. Hayes Crawford had been out the day the explosion happened.

During the investigation into the cause of the fire, several illegal guns and some keys to storage units had survived the blaze, leading police to Hayes' drug manufacturing operations and his subsequent arrest. I'd celebrated Hayes' fifteen-years' sentencing by taking the pins out of my ever-present braided bun. I never wore my hair in that tight, severe style again.

As far as I know, the explosion only exposed Hayes' storage units, not how he'd operated his drug exchanges. But Hayes is in prison. If he is somehow behind this distribution of Bliss, he's deviously clever to have partnered with a college professor, not to mention moving his drug distribution uptown to a much higher paying clientele. If it's not Hayes, it's someone who knew the ins and outs of his organization in the past. Either way, renewed anger bolsters my determination. "I'll do my best to make him pay, Mina."

Ten minutes later, I open Mina's door, my red cape swirling around me as I step out of the way. Mina buzzes out of the room dressed in a full-out woodland fairy costume, complete with iridescent see-through wings.

Sebastian is leaning against the opposite wall, arms crossed over his chest. He quickly catches Mina when she throws herself into his arms. "Scarlett was exactly what I needed to crawl out of my dark hole. Thank you for being such a jerk, Seb."

Barking a laugh, he sets her down, then adjusts her mask. "I'm happy to be a bastard for you any time. And you're welcome."

She frowns. "I really hate it when you talk like that."

He shrugs, unaffected by her chiding. "You off to the party?"

She nods, her curled hair bobbing. "Just for a little while. I want to thank my friends who came to support me."

Turning to me, she reaches for my hand. "Come downstairs with me, Scarlett. I'd like you to meet some of my friends."

I'd watched the exchange between Mina and Sebastian with confusion. They seem close, yet not somehow. I can't say why I get that impression, but it's there, just under the surface.

When she laces our fingers together, I exhale a quiet breath of relief and clasp hers. "I'd love to meet your friends." Once I'm downstairs and she's distracted socializing with her buddies, I'll find Cass and we'll sneak out of the party before Sebastian can catch up to me.

Mina and I don't take more than a few steps before he snags my other hand. "You go on downstairs, Mina. Scarlett and I have something to discuss first."

## CHAPTER FIVE

"*B*ut, Seb—" Mina pouts.

"Go, Mina."

She shoots him an annoyed look, then squeezes my hand and smiles. "See you downstairs, okay?"

"Sure," I say quietly, then gulp back my nerves as she walks off down the hall.

Once she rounds the corner and then closes the door behind her, Sebastian tugs my hand and starts walking. "Where are we going?" I ask, putting on the brakes.

He frowns when we grind to a halt, my heels digging into the plush carpet. "Somewhere we can talk."

I shake my head, my stomach knotting. "I really need to be going. Ca—um, Yvette is going to be wondering where I am."

He glances down at our hands, where I'm desperately trying to twist free of his hold, but he's just too strong. His mesmerizing eyes snap back to me. "We had a deal. You got to see Mina in exchange for answering how you know me."

I shrug. "There's really nothing to tell. I don't know you, Mr. Black."

"Sebastian. Now that you know my name, use it," he says, his voice low, clipped.

I lift my chin slightly, feeling as if I've been reprimanded. "Fine. I don't know you, *Sebastian*. Now that I've answered your question, will you please release my hand so I can leave."

His eyes narrow. "I don't believe you."

"I don't care if you believe me or not. It's the truth." I poke him in the chest for emphasis. "I. Don't. Know. You."

"Liar," he says silkily, hooking his finger around mine just as I lift it from his chest. "Which means we're not done yet," he finishes, yanking me toward him.

I'm so surprised, I stumble forward, but before I can recover, he quickly scoops me up, carrying me off through a door to his left and then down another hall.

"Put me down," I hiss through gritted teeth while trying to buck out of his hold, but his arms are like bands of steel. When he carries me through a partially open door into what appears to be a study/library with low lit sconces, a huge dark desk, and brimming bookshelves, then kicks the door closed behind us, I yell, "This is fucking kidnapping!"

Setting me down, he folds his arms over his chest, blocking my only exit. "And you're the one *fucking* trespassing."

His voice is strangely even as I whirl to face him, but it's the calmness in it that scares me. It tells me he has the patience to wait all night to get the answers he wants.

"You can start by telling me your name."

I fold my arms, matching his stance. "It's Scarlett."

"Your real name," he counters, an edge to his voice.

Good. So he's not as calm as he lets on. "Why does that matter?"

He scowls. "So I can hunt you down if you try to screw Mina in any way."

Pushing my hair over my shoulder, I snort. "If she can trust me, then you should too."

"Why should I?"

"Because you love her and trust her judgment," I say quietly, calming down.

"I do love her." His mouth twists ironically. "Though I'm not so sure about her judgment. We wouldn't be here discussing this if it were sound."

The fact I was right about him loving her twists in my gut, hitting me hard. It's like the image of that hero I'd held onto for so long—the dream man who wouldn't abandon me, take advantage of me, or disappoint me—

had finally dissipated. Like all dreams eventually do when you finally wake up.

"We all make mistakes." I lift my chin slightly, shrugging off thoughts about my own past. "I only want to help her."

"I thought this was just a story to you," he says, full of cynicism.

"It was, but I'd rather help Mina if I can."

"Why?"

"She reminds me of someone I knew, well...who she could've been. And I understand the sadness she's feeling."

He lowers his arms and steps forward to touch my jaw, his tone softening. "Why won't you tell me your name?"

The sensation of his fingers tracing my jawline, caressing me so tenderly, sends chills down my spine, which just isn't fair. I smack his hand away and side-step him. "What are you doing? You shouldn't touch me like that." I frown at him warily as he turns with me. I take a backward step toward the door.

"Touch you like what?" He steps forward, forcing me to step back. He continues stalking me until my back is against the door. Resting one hand on the door beside my head, he stares down at me, his gaze slowly sliding to my mouth and then back to my eyes. "Like this?"

When he trails his fingers along my jaw and then

down my neck, my whole body starts to shake. "Like you want me. You shouldn't do that."

"You want this. I hear it in your voice, feel it in the way you react to my touch."

I shake my head and glance away. "You're with someone else. It's not right, Sebastian."

He clasps my jaw, forcing me to meet his gaze. "Who am I with?"

"Um, Mina. She slips your mind awfully fast."

When Sebastian lets out an amused laugh, I tense and try to slide away from him.

He lowers his hand to my shoulder, keeping me locked in place with a firm grip. "Not so fast. You really don't know anything about me, do you?"

When I grit my teeth and shake my head, he slowly rubs his thumb along the side of my neck. "Mina is my sister."

All I can do is gape. None of my research of the Blake family mentioned a third son. My thoughts must've scrolled across my face, because the look in his eyes is both amused and mocking.

"I really *am* a bastard. The dark skeleton in Adam Blake's family closet, with no official claim to the Blake fortune. To society I don't exist, a black sheep who only inherits if he keeps his mouth shut. I might not be blood out there," he jerks his head toward the window, "But I don't mind yanking on familial strings when the mood suits me."

Hooking his finger on my chin, he slides his thumb sensually across my lips, then continues in an ironic tone, "I'm a fucking walking cliché, Scarlett."

"Why—why are you telling me this? You don't know me. How can you trust me with something like that?" He has to know this information would shove Mina's to the back page, not just for our school paper but news across the country. Everyone knows who the Blakes are. Their massive wealth is well known, but apparently Sebastian has been a very well kept dirty secret. Had his father had an affair? And where does he fall in the birth order, between Damien and Gavin? My guess is older.

"But somehow you know me." Raking his hand through his hair, he lets out a hoarse laugh. "You gained Mina's trust, which is no small feat. I told you my secret because I want you to trust me with yours."

I quickly shake my head. "I—I don't have any secrets."

Bending close, he whispers in my ear, "Liar. You get one more chance to tell me something about you."

"Or what? You'll punish me?" I laugh. When he presses a warm kiss along my neck, murmuring his assent, my insides quiver. I set my hands against his hard chest, savoring the rock hard muscle flexing under my hands. "I'm too old to spank."

Sebastian grasps my waist and tugs me flush against his hard body. "I'm fully aware you're all woman." His voice is a rasping symphony of deep, seductive tones playing against every nerve ending in my body as he slides his hands down the curve of my hips to palm my ass. Clasping me closer, he presses his erection against my center, his voice dropping to an even deeper baritone. "But you're never too old to spank."

Loving his aggressiveness, I flex my fingers against the soft leather fabric covering his chest. "Well then, it's a good thing I haven't done anything worth punishing."

"That's a matter of perspective." Lifting his mesmerizing dual gaze to mine, he holds our aroused bodies together like critical game pieces waiting to be played. My body clenches in anticipation as he slowly slides his thumb along the curve of my ass. "Since I'm in a sharing mood, there's one more thing you should know about me. I'm a man of my word."

"I don't doubt it." I'm not exactly sure where he's going with this, but with each leisurely stroke of his thumb along my skin, my body temperature rises. I'm getting wetter by the second.

"Give me a word that means safety to you. Just one word," he says.

*That's an odd request.* Without thinking, I blurt out the first word that comes to mind. "Rainbow."

His thumb stops moving and his eyebrows shoot up behind the mask. "Interesting choice."

*That was stupid, Talia!* I immediately tense and hope he doesn't make the connection.

He palms my ass once more, his expression serious. "Use it if you need it. Got it?"

*Need it for what?* I'm so relieved he doesn't make the connection, I start to nod, then gasp in outrage when he moves with lightning speed, landing a resounding smack against my butt cheek.

"What the hell! My thin dress and underwear did nothing to soften the sting. I try to jerk free, but he's immovable.

"That's for ditching me earlier," he grates, then says in a quieter tone, "Say your safe word, Scarlett, and I'll end this now."

"Let go!" I grit out, shocked that my bolting bothered him, but also by my own response to the hot fire on my ass zinging its way through me. When his hand traces the curve of my ass, his fingers sliding under my panties, I freeze. He strokes away the pain, kneading my flesh tenderly. Time seems to stand still, my heart thrumming at the sensation of his thumb sliding the edge of my panties back, exposing my cheek fully. I'm so turned on, yet I can't decide whether to punch him or kiss him.

Another smack. "That's for lying to me."

My anger quickly ignites once more. This time I

hammer my fist on his muscular arm, trying to break free, but he's just too strong. "I haven't lied to you," I hiss. *I don't know you. I don't trust you. I don't trust anyone. I wish I did. I wish things were different. I wish my past was different.*

He grabs my ass like he owns it, massaging my skin with enticing, possessive strokes. When he slides his hand lower to the back of my thigh and along the curve of my ass, teasing the edge of my panties, his fingers so close, but not touching me, I fight back the moan rising in my throat. As the sting fades, his sexy voice sends shivers down my spine. "You can call this quits whenever you want. Just say the word."

*Safe word.* I get it now. His comment is so seductively intriguing, it's hard to know if he's seducing me, challenging me, or prepping me for more punishment of some other transgression. Sure I can say, "Rainbow" to make him stop, but there's a part of me that wants to know what *this* is between us. What else have I done to elicit such heated intensity from him? Instead of playing by his rules, I decide to give his frustration back to him in my own way. Grabbing a fistful of his hair, I yank hard. "Screw you!"

Exhaling a harsh grunt, he digs his fingers into my rear, his piercing gaze narrowing to a sharp edge. I squeeze my eyes shut and tighten my butt muscles, preparing as he bends close to speak in a steely tone against my cheek. "And this is for waiting until fucking *now* to walk into my life."

I gasp in shock when his mouth captures mine in a bone-melting kiss. The second he jerks me impossibly close, molding me to him like a second skin, my adrenaline spikes, setting me on fire.

His sensual spanking must have revved me up. Or maybe it's just everything about Sebastian, from his seductive words, to his intense stare, to his thrilling, territorial hold on my body. *What did he mean by that last comment? And why does he sound furious and regretful at the same time?* I shake off my jumbled thoughts and clasp his neck, tugging him as close as I can. I've had eight years of build-up thinking about this glorious man, and I'm not letting him go yet.

Sebastian groans against my mouth, then slides his tongue aggressively against mine, provoking a response. Its electrifying effect zings all the way to the bottoms of my feet. Just as I twine my tongue with his, he starts to delve deeper, but then he pulls back, his face tense with frustration. "Give me something. Anything."

The plea in his voice speaks to that same desperate feeling I've carried around with me since I was a little girl. Crossing paths with him when I was thirteen shined a tiny ray of hope in a life that was crashing down around me. In my heart and mind, he's been "the one" for eight years, a fantasy I never expected to happen. I'd given him many names in my past imaginings, but Sebastian makes my insides burn.

I love it. The name fits him so well.

And now that my life is in an upward trajectory, I want the one man—whose brief appearance in my life meant more than any other—to be the person who helps me hold onto the belief he'd started all those years ago—that I was worth the effort. Until I met him that day, I'd always felt like no one cared. My aunt was the only one who loved me, because she had to. No one else had. Not my mother, not my father, not Walt, not Hayes. No one.

"Tell me your name," he rasps against my skin, trailing warm lips down my neck.

I know tonight is all we'll have, so I'm going to make the most of it before he disappears from my life again. Wrapping my arms around his neck, I press against him and shake my head. "No names tonight. Remember."

He fists his hand in my hair, tugging slightly so I have to meet his gaze. "You know mine."

"I didn't ask you."

He scowls, hating that answer.

Pressing my lips to his neck, I trail them up his jaw. "I'll give you something better."

He grunts and captures my chin with his thumb. "I want your name."

The sconce lights flicker, then die out completely,

shrouding us in darkness. Thunder booms, shaking the room.

I lick my lips and offer him a choice. "You can either have my name or me."

With his back to the window, his face is in the shadows. Mine flashes in and out with the lightning, but I feel his fingers flexing on my hip and hear his sharp intake of breath. He wasn't expecting that.

Heart pounding, I make it perfectly clear what I'm offering. "My name or my body. You choose." Once it's out there, I hold my breath. I don't know if he'll take it or toss me aside, he's so freaking domineering and hard to read.

Tilting my chin higher, he feathers his fingers down my throat, then tugs the bow, unraveling the cape from around my neck.

When it whooshes to the floor at my feet, I exhale slowly, relieved that he's chosen not to ask.

# CHAPTER SIX

My skin prickles as he traces his fingers across the curve of my breast above the corset, then dips a finger between my cleavage, a territorial smile tilting his lips. "In giving yourself to me, you've agreed to let me do anything I want to you. I'm not tender, Scarlett. I'm demanding. I like control. I'm all about the physical...and the release."

"So you're saying you don't make love."

"I fuck..." he answers in a matter-of-fact tone, then slowly traces a finger along my jaw, "But always with pleasure as the ultimate payoff. In exchange, I promise you'll come until you beg me to stop, and even then I just might not."

Lightning flashes along the side of his face, reflecting a quick, wicked smile.

While he promises a rough romp, he gently slides his thumbs across my breasts, then slowly begins to unhook each of the corset's hooks from its matching eyelet.

"And my safe word?" I ask breathlessly.

He pauses, glancing up from the hooks. "Use it if you must." Holding my gaze, he takes his time freeing the last few hooks. "But you won't."

*Is that a challenge or a promise?* My belly flutters in excitement, while my mind tries to reconcile his aggressive sexual statements with his tender attentiveness. It's such an arousing contrast, my insides feel like they might combust. The second my corset falls to the floor, a flood of arousal swells my freed breasts, slamming straight to my nipples. I hold back the whimper at the near painful pressure, not wanting him to know just how much he affects me. Even the cotton dress is chaffing the hard pink tips; they're that sensitive.

I gasp when he steps right up to me, his voice a sensual rumble vibrating against my chest. "I'll have your name by the end of the night," he says, confident, assured. "I just wanted you to offer it willingly."

Does that mean he thinks I'll give him my name *unwillingly?* Good luck, bud. I don't get a chance to wonder as he slides his hands up my waist to capture my nipples between his thumbs and forefingers. The dress does little to dull the effect as he pinches with enough force to make me cry out in a haze of pleasure/pain.

When he doesn't release me right away, but continues to apply steady, frustrating pressure, I began to throb deep in my core. It's an achy, painful, I'll-need-a-release-soon kind of throbbing. I grip his hard biceps and begin to pant, my legs trembling.

When I try to press my legs together to stop the torturous pulsing, he quickly slides his knee between mine, breaking my thighs apart. The barest tease of his hard thigh muscle brushes against my aching center as he dips his head to whisper huskily in my ear. "There are so many other ways to punish."

The second I move close to his thigh, hoping to apply pressure where I need it most, he pulls his leg out of my reach. I bite the inside of my cheek and quickly realize I'm in way over my head.

"So beautifully fucking responsive," he murmurs, rolling his thumbs across my nipples. "Your name," he commands.

I shake my head, then gasp hard when he drags his thumbs down the front of my nipples. Even through the material, unimaginable pleasure sweeps through me.

"You're going to come while standing. I won't touch you anywhere but here. You can't move. Don't touch anything but my arms. Got it?"

"But I don't think I can—" I exhale raggedly as pleasure shifts to pain, radiating throughout my chest. He'd only applied the slightest pressure at a different angle, but the effect is enough to cut me off.

"Don't think. Just take direction."

I frown; I don't like being told what to do, but his voice softens to a silky purr. "The payoff will be worth it."

When I slowly nod, he smiles, and I finally see the dimple on his cheek for the first time. It's barely there, but still perceptible. What changed in his life since I met him that night? I don't think the man before me has looked for rainbows in a long time. He's too focused, too intense, too...dark. *Black as sin*, he'd said. I want to ask him so much, but I can't, not without revealing myself. Damn him for being this sexy and seductively intriguing.

He moves his thumbs once more, doing something new that makes my legs feel boneless and my eyes shutter to half-mast. This time I can't hold back my moan. I'm shocked to feel my inner muscles flexing, coiling, ready for release. I take a quick breath through my nose.

"Not yet." He shakes his head.

My eyes widen. "Why not?"

Desire flashes in his eyes, swift and heated. "I'm going to tell you what I'm going to do to you first, then when I let you, you can come."

*When he lets me? Screw that.* My mind instantly plans a revolt, while he bends close to my ear, his warm breath rushing across my skin, his voice beautifully rough. "Are you wet for me right now? It makes me harder just thinking about you dripping with want, soaking through your clothes."

When I don't answer, he tweaks my nipples and a shudder overtakes me. I shake my head, too stubborn to tell him how much I want this. *Two can play at this game, Mr. Black.*

He nips my earlobe. "I can't wait to taste you. My mouth is watering just thinking about rolling you across my tongue, savoring your flavor...lapping you up. Every last drop."

My stomach clenches and moisture gathers, intensifying the steady throb between my legs. I'm so freaking turned on, I bow my head and inhale steady, even breaths trying to hold out longer than him.

"Tell me, damn it!" he demands, his thumbnails brushing across the very tips of my nipples.

I whimper, then bite out angrily, "Yes, I'm *sopping*. Are you happy?"

"Miss Scarlett, I'm *raging*," he admits, his voice gruffer than it was a second ago.

His honest admission makes me smile, so I turn the tables on him, lifting my head to whisper in his ear, "I'm tighter than you've ever had. That I can promise you."

"Fuck me," he utters, his head snapping up, eyes blazing with lust. Rolling my nipples between his fingers, he tugs just enough. "I'm going to pound into your sweet body over and over, filling you full of what you want most. Me. Come *now*."

The sexy words are barely out of his mouth before I'm screaming through the orgasm roaring through me. Pulses of hot and cold tremors slide up and down my body, taking away my ability to stand through the all-consuming experience.

He catches me when I crumple, lifting me into his arms. Cradling me to his chest, he presses a kiss to my forehead, then carries me out of the library and down the hall in determined strides. His hold on me is fiercely tight as we enter another room, this one darker than the library, quieter.

A bedroom.

My body is still clenching and thrumming from the aftereffects of my climax as he lays me on the bed. He tugs my first boot off, then the second. His movements are swift, purposeful, like nothing will stop the gale force about to rush over me.

Thunder booms outside, punctuating his actions, and I welcome every bit of his primitive fury. Bending forward, he surprises me when he slowly runs the tips of his fingers high along my leg before he begins to slide my thigh-high hose off. With each section of skin he exposes, he pauses to press a kiss, first, to my inner thigh, then the inside of my knee, and finally along the sensitive side of my ankle.

Moving to my other leg, his fingers brush much higher on my thigh, causing my breathing to stall. As he makes his way down my leg, he applies light kisses in slightly different areas before removing the second hose completely. My body's clenching in renewed arousal by the time he's done.

Straightening, he takes off his bow and quiver, then his belt and shirt. His breathing saws in and out as he stares down at me for a beat before removing his mask. I'm glad to know I'm not the only one affected by his attentive removal of my hose.

The outline of his broad shoulders and hard, fit body make me want to explore every dip and hollow with my tongue. I'm sad that it's too dark to see more than bits of light play on his face from trees moving in the wind outside, but that means he can't really see mine either.

I reach up and remove my mask. I want to kiss him without it in the way. I don't want anything between us. We'll just hide in the shadows instead.

"Your name," he says, his tone demanding compliance.

I pull my dress over my head, tossing it to him.

My answer.

He crushes the material in a tight fist, then drops it to

the floor. Reaching for my ankles, he encircles them, fingers flexing on my skin. Distant lightning flashes, briefly highlighting the top half of his face. The room goes dark again, and all I can picture is the near feral look in his amazing eyes as he tugs me toward him with a powerful jerk, his tone gravelly and full of want. "Then I'll just call you *Mine*."

When he runs his hands up the inside of my thighs, pressing them to the bed with a quiet order, "Keep them here," I comply, eager anticipation curling in my belly. I'm exposed, but he's already seen the ugliest side of me. When I was raw and at my weakest. He just doesn't know it.

He slowly runs his nose up my wet panties, groaning low in his throat. I swallow as he inhales, then lets out a dark growl of pleasure. "Your scent is driving me insane."

He doesn't touch me where I want him to though. Instead he runs his tongue along the edge of my underwear, the erotic sensation of his warmth so close but not hitting where I need him to puts me just shy of wanting to scream.

I start to touch his dark hair, to direct him where I want him to go, but he jerks his head up and shakes it. "Keep your hands on the bed if you want me to make you come."

Gritting my teeth, I clutch the soft bedcovers underneath me, regretting that I can't dig my fingers into the thick, silky mass. *Is it as soft as it looks? What does it smell like?*

He grunts his approval, then presses his thumbs on either side of my entrance, opening my lips wider. I moan as he tugs my underwear slightly, pulling the cloth inside me. The brief brush against my clit makes me throb.

Then he runs his tongue along the sensitive skin he's exposed, so close but still not touching me. "You're not hitting the right spot," I say, my body clenching, needing friction.

He chuckles and slides his hands under my butt. "Is this what you want?" The feel of his tongue flattened along my underwear, lapping all the way up, makes my hips buck.

"You're so sweet," he murmurs, pressing his nose inside me and inhaling through my wet panties like he can't get enough.

His act is so primal and arousing, my insides flex, desire pulsating. "Then taste me, damn it!" I demand, sounding frantic...desperate for him.

He slides his tongue past the underwear, flicking it briefly inside me. I roll my hips and gasp.

"Say you're mine," he rumbles.

He doesn't have to ask me twice. I'm already his. "I'm yours."

Letting out a deep sound of masculine satisfaction,

he pulls back slightly then rips my underwear right off my body. I don't care. My hips are moving on their own at this point.

When he puts my underwear in his mouth and sucks and groans, while his eyes bore into me, I want to rip that damned material from his lips. Jealous, I'm nearly delirious with the need to feel his mouth on *me*. Belatedly I realize I'm blubbering for him to taste me, damn it. *What is he doing to me? I can't even think straight.*

"I'm going to," he promises. Dropping my panties on the floor, he bends down and runs his warm tongue across my slit and all the way up.

The second he latches onto my clit, I scream out in pleasure, pressing myself wantonly against his hot mouth. I want everything he can give and more.

He growls low in his throat and grips my ass, delving his tongue deep inside. When I try to wrap my legs around his neck, to pull him closer, he stops and lifts his head. "Down on the bed."

"But—"

A dark eyebrow arches. "Did you give yourself to me?"

When I swallow reflexively, then nod, a darkly seductive smile tilts his lips. "Then take what I give and trust me."

I do trust him, so I sigh and let my legs fall back to the bed in complete surrender.

As soon as I yield in his hands, he swipes his tongue inside me again, then swallows and goes back for more, groaning his approval against my body, "Fucking hell, you taste better the more aroused you get. I could dine on your sweet pussy all night long."

My heart rate rockets. I whimper and try to push closer, needing more.

"Is this what you want?" he says, sliding a finger deep inside at the same time he captures my clit between his lips, giving it a brief tug.

I pant and arch against him. "Yes, more."

He adds another finger, then slides them both in and out of me, exhaling his own groan. "Damn, you're tight as hell."

"No surprise there," I mutter with a half laugh. When he suddenly stops moving and lifts his head to stare at me, I tense. "What?"

"Are you...is this your first time?"

I bite my lip and nod, wanting him to know I'd chosen him on purpose.

Apparently that was the wrong response, because he abruptly withdraws his fingers and stands up at the end of the bed, jamming shaky hands through his hair.

"What the fuck?" Pacing a couple of times, he halts and growls toward the ceiling, "Why would you do that?"

He sounds so angry, his mood so mercurial, I scoot

back on the bed, resting my back against the pillows. "I'd hoped my enthusiasm would override my lack of experience. I guess that's not the case."

Facing me, his hands fist by his sides. "You should be with someone else. I don't deserve this."

"It was my offer to make," I say, his words twisting my heart.

He shakes his head in fast jerks. "Not to me."

It's like he believes he's undeserving. That can't be further from the truth. "I want *you*." *It's always been you.*

"Why?"

His voice is full of angst and banked desire, so I answer him honestly, throwing his words from earlier back at him. "You stand out. There's definitely something about you."

He sits down on the bed, sliding his thumb across my ankle, as if he can't *not* touch me. "I want you so bad my balls ache, but your first time should be with someone who—"

"Knows how to make me scream?" I interrupt. "A man who knows every erogenous zone on the female body and exactly how to get me off? Why *wouldn't* I want that for my first time? I might be a virgin, but I'm far from innocent, Sebastian." *Trust me, I'm as undeserving as you think you are, but I can't help but wish for more anyway.*

His thumb slows on my ankle, his fingers curling around the arch of my foot. "I can make it memorable."

My heart trips, hope filling my chest, making my pulse race all over again. "Are you going to finish what you started?"

"Say it again," he says, moving his hand up my foot, pressing his thumb along the arch.

My blood rushes in my ears. I'm afraid to move. Afraid to breathe. "What do you want me to say?"

"Tell me you're mine."

"I'm yours, Sebastian. All yours."

Snarling his agreement, he grips my foot and slides me across the bed with one powerful tug until we're nose to nose. "Your name..." he begins. Wrapping my leg around his hip, he slides his hand all the way up my thigh, gripping me in a possessive hold. "If I'm going to be your first, the least you can do is tell me that."

Our breaths take over each other. Both of us pant with need, sexual tension arcing between us in invisible bolts of electricity. "I'm Red."

His mouth thins, frustration emanating from his stiffening shoulders.

I cup his jaw, smoothing the ticking muscle there. "And you're Black. Together we're passion. You were right about that—"

He claims my mouth, the press of his lips cutting off

my words. Fingers spear through my hair, holding me tight, as if he's afraid I'll try to escape.

I curl my leg tighter around him, pulling myself into his lap, but he quickly changes our position, his muscular chest pressing me back against the bed.

While he kisses me senseless, his hands are everywhere, cupping my thighs, hooking them around his hips. He rocks his erection against me, creating glorious friction. I mewl and gyrate my hips under him.

"You are so beautiful," he rasps against my mouth. Just as I clutch him close, he quickly clasps my hands and pulls them over my head, holding my wrists with one hand.

While I inhale deeply, he presses his hardness against my sex and dips his head to capture one of my jutting nipples in his mouth.

I gasp and writhe under him, needing more.

He moves to my other breast, sucking a bit harder, jacking my arousal.

"Your pants," I say breathlessly, bucking underneath him. "Take them off."

He lets out a restrained chuckle. "You're a live wire. Let me build your desire." Bending close to my ear, his voice is velvet sliding across my skin. "It'll be worth it, Little Red. I promise. I'm going to release your hands, but I want you to keep them above your head. Don't touch me."

I try to keep my hands where he leaves them, but the second he rubs his thumbs along the sides of my breasts, I quickly grip his shoulders, breathing out, "I want to touch you. Every part of you."

Jerking a heated gaze to mine, his shadowed expression intensifies, his nostrils flaring. He exhales harshly, "Not yet."

When I don't immediately remove my hands, he backs up. I'm surprised to see a pleased smile curve his lips just before he turns away to grab something from the floor.

"Scoot back some," he commands, setting his knee on the bed.

I eye the soft leather strap in his hand, recognizing his belt from his costume. My heart trips, but I do as he asks.

"Raise your hands above your head."

When I don't immediately obey, he lays the strap across my breasts, then slowly slides the material across my nipples, turning it so the rougher edge trails along the sensitized tips. I suck in a breath, then narrow my gaze. "I won't be tied."

"You've proven you have no will power," he says on an arrogant purr.

When I snap my chin up, ready to deny his statement, he cuts me off, his tone calmly even. "Do I have to tell you again?" But it's his eyes that make my breath whoosh out in an excited huff. There's nothing laidback about the light and dark orbs staring back at me. They're pinning me to the bed already, mimicking the tension in his shoulders. He's a panther, waiting to strike if I dare defy him.

And I so want to be devoured, so I lift my arms.

Grunting his approval, he crawls over me and quickly wraps my wrists, tying them to the wooden slats on the headboard behind me.

Not about to be completely overruled, before he moves away, I press my lips to the hard muscle along his inner thigh.

He inhales a quick breath, then shifts with lightning speed, his hands capturing my jaw. Crouched over me, he tugs me half off the bed, his big body surrounding me in steely muscle and dominant magnetism as he captures my lips in a devouring kiss.

My chest wedged between his corded thighs, I feel every bit of his hard heat. I kiss him back with just as much feverish passion until I'm shaking with longing all over again.

He breaks our kiss and rests his forehead to mine. Our breaths commingling, hearts pounding, I tug on the belt binding me. "Are you sure you want my hands tied? I can think of at least one place I want to wrap my fingers around."

"Minx," he rasps, biting my bottom lip before he releases me to slide down my body.

I nurse my swollen bottom lip between my teeth and watch his hands glide over my skin, my breathing hitching in anticipation. When he pinches my nipples once more, I arch my back and moan at the arousing sensations building inside me. With a dark smile, he prowls back up my body and tilts my chin. As he alternately licks and nips his way down my neck, along my chest, then past my navel, I start to quiver all over, I want him between my legs so bad.

Once his warm mouth finally hovers over my sex, I keen, but force myself to still. My body bowed tight, back arched, I wait for him to connect where I want him most. The second he grabs my hips in a possessive hold and latches onto my clit, sucking hard, I let out a shuddering, hissing breath and rock my hips against his delicious onslaught.

"Like that, do you?" he teases, burying two fingers inside me.

Tears streak down my temples. I moan, my body taut and vibrating its need for release. His masculine scent lingers in my nose. I inhale deeply, trying to draw every part of him in as he masterfully slides his fingers in and out of my body. "I'm going to hurt you if I don't prime you first. Understand?"

There's something incredibly heartwarming and

seductively sexy about the volatile pulsing of his attentions from fierce possessor to tender lover then back again while his hot breath bathes my sex. Everything about him heightens my senses, teasing me even more. I nod in response, near frantic for him to take all of me fully into his mouth.

When he adds another finger at the same time he teases my clit with his teeth, my legs start to quiver. "Oh God. Oh, God. I'm going to—"

"Not yet," he says harshly. He stills his hand and moves to plant a soft kiss where my leg meets my body.

I whimper and dig my heels into the covers, trying to get him to give me what I want. Tender kisses bathe up my inner thigh, then down toward my sex but not touching. Finally I get it. He's waiting for me to calm down.

The second my hips settle on the bed, he moves back to kissing and sucking on my clit while his fingers plunder and tease, exploring every part of me. Again and again, he does this until my head is thrashing, my body is quaking, and I'm near incoherent with need.

As waves of heat flush my skin, I beg him, "Please, please, Sebastian."

"What do you want?" he asks, his voice calm and controlled. He slows the sensual glide of his fingers inside me, then withdraws, his movements now a teeth-grinding unhurried pace. Sweat beads between my breasts. My skin feels too tight on my body, all prickly and warm.

"Let me come!" I demand through clenched teeth.

"That's my girl," he says in a smug tone before latching onto my clit with a ravenous ferocity he hadn't used before.

I scream his name as all the raging tension building in my body unfurls in spasms of pleasurable, mind-numbing contractions. I might be tied to the bed, but I feel intimately tethered to his hands and mouth, like I'm floating in a surreal dream I never want to wake from.

Once I stop panting, he gives me one more long, lingering lick, then quickly stands to kick off his shoes and shuck out of his pants. When he reaches inside the nightstand to grab a condom, my gaze locks on his hands while he rolls the protection down his very impressive erection.

The second he sets his knee on the bed, I scoot back, tugging on the belt to sit up. He's massive. Both thick and long. He puts BOB to shame by at least three inches. *Oh shit!* "You're too big," I strangle out, worried he's going to split me in two.

Reaching over, he effortlessly pushes my fingers out of the way, tugs one end of the belt, and the whole thing comes undone, releasing me. Before I can ponder his expertise with magical knots, he clasps my wrist and pulls my hand toward his erection. "You will take all of me."

I experience a moment of panic, expecting him to wrap my fingers around his cock, but when he releases my hand just as the tips of my fingers touch him, I relax. The trust I feel for this man melts my heart, rocking me to the core. Taking a breath, I revel in the heaviness lifting off my chest the moment I slide my fingers around him. I love that he's giving me free rein. When he shudders and groans, I flex my fingers, enjoying the fact I can make him feel as deeply.

Biting my lip, I start to slide my thumb over the rounded tip, but he lifts my chin and bends close to capture my mouth in another devastating kiss, whispering against my lips, "You'll be begging me for every inch soon, Little Red."

# CHAPTER SEVEN

*T*he thought of connecting with him like this overrides my apprehension, and my fingers reflexively tighten around him. He bites my bottom lip again, exhaling a deep groan as his hips flex forward. "Lay back," he says, his words almost guttural.

Leaning over me, he slides a seductive kiss along my jaw as he eases the head of his cock inside me. When he pulls back slightly, I exhale an unsteady breath. That wasn't so bad. I lift my hips, encouraging him to continue.

He shakes his head. "Take it slow."

I flatten my hands on his hard pectorals, loving the feel of his muscles flexing under my palms. Running my hands past his wide shoulders, I clasp his neck to pull him to me for another kiss.

His fierce eyes snap to mine for a second before he kisses me, his tongue hungrily swiping inside my mouth, swirling against mine, thrusting deep...pillaging me. My whole body tightens in blissful response.

I moan against his mouth and lift my hips again. I trace my nails down his back, thrilled that he's finally letting me touch him. He's sculpted in all the ways that make my mouth water, slabs of defined muscle and sinew flexing with each move he makes.

This time he slides deeper and I let out a low, pleased moan, enjoying the sting of my body resisting his girth. Slowly, ever so slowly, my muscles give way a fraction at a time.

His breathing ramps and his hips flex forward, moving deeper. "Holy shit! You're so fucking tight."

Rock hard arms strain over me, his body a tight bow, arching, ready to release. I hate that he's holding back. I surge upward, forcing him to take me.

Swallowing my yelp of pain, I tense for a second. I can't help it. Damn that hurt, but in a good burn kind of way.

He completely stills and curses under his breath. "Why did you...are you okay?"

When he doesn't move, just stays buried deep, the heat of his balls teasing my sex, I flex my muscles, tightening my walls around him. "I'm not made of glass,

Sebastian. I want to see you unleashed, to be yourself with me. I want you to *fuck me*."

A hiss escapes his mouth and the beautiful planes of his face harden. He's on the edge. Leaning down, he runs his nose along my cheek before he husks next to my ear, "You're going to feel me tomorrow. When you pee, you'll burn. When you sit, you'll squirm. When you cross your legs, you'll throb. Every movement will be uncomfortable, and you'll know I was here." To punctuate his point, he surges even deeper, taking my breath.

"Is that what you want?" he sounds shocked and hopeful and intrigued all at once.

I hook my hands behind his neck and slowly nod. "If I don't have a hard time sitting for at least three days, you didn't do it hard enough." His breathing ramps as I trail my fingers through his thick hair and hold his gaze. "I always bet on black. Now make it memorable."

"Think you can match me?" he challenges as he withdraws, then slowly eases back inside, setting an unhurried pace.

I move my hips in tandem to his, pleasure building all over. He counters my movements, his hand sliding to my ass. Gripping me tight, a growl rumbles from deep in his chest right before he slams inside me in one hard, powerful thrust.

I scream out as my orgasm roars past the swift pain in

my core, pleasure shooting from my sex straight to my chest. Clenching and contracting, my body fists tight around him, wanting to milk him, but he's not done. Not at all.

His breathing rushes out in harsh, rampant gusts as he slides his hand to my thigh and hitches it high around his hip, giving him better access.

When he surges into me this time, I swear I see stars, the jarring pleasure radiates all the way to my scalp. I dig my nails into his back, and with one heel anchored on his hard ass and the other pressed into the soft bed, I meet each of his thrusts with my own.

"That's it, Red," he grates out. "Damn, you feel so good. My own fucking beautiful wet dream."

I know I'm going to be sore for a while. And I'll probably have bruises. His grip on my ass and hip is beyond bruising. He's just so freaking big, his body incredibly powerful, like steel covered in skin. But I don't care. I welcome the onslaught and rake my nails down his back to encourage his thorough taking. "That's two days, not three," I taunt through my own panting.

He roars, then grabs my other leg and pushes them both up to his hips as he thrusts hard, pounding into me.

This time my scream is a bit of pleasure and pain. The new position allows him much deeper access, and I know I'm definitely going to have a hard time sitting comfortably for a while.

Sweat drips off his face, sliding down my chest, but

all I can feel is heat and want. Delicious, toe-curling anticipation builds, tightening my belly and lower muscles.

The second my next orgasm hits, he grunts out against my throat, "Take me. All of me," before he pumps his body deeper and deeper. He's relentless, continuing to overwhelm me, hitting on nerves I never knew I had. And I do take all of him, shocked that my desire starts to build all over again. He doesn't stop until I come once more, arching against him, crying out his name. Only then does he let out a deep growl of satisfaction and collapses on top of me in a masculine heap of muscle and warmth.

I lay there, a bit dazed as he cups the back of my head and presses his forehead to mine. When our breathing slows, he runs his nose across my cheek, leaving tender kisses along the way. "Mine," he says in my ear, then he leans over to reach for the tissue box on the nightstand.

Before I can move, he turns and gathers me against his big frame. Tucking my back in the cradle of his body, he wraps his arm around my waist and locks me in place.

As we lay together, listening to the rain, the sports watch on the nightstand lights up, flashing one eleven. A couple seconds of worry flickers when he starts to lean over me. The glow is illuminating my whole face.

But he just touches a button on the watch and the

room goes dark once more. Exhaling quietly, I ask, "Is this your room?"

He settles back into place and traces his fingers up my hip. "I stay in here, yes."

Mina's room is decorated like any other young woman's living space, with bright pillows on her bed and matching curtains. Posters line her walls and trophies and dance pictures litter her desk. A lifetime of memories. It looks lived in. In contrast, his room resembles a hotel with its bare walls and only a watch, a phone, and a few toiletries on the nightstand.

"But you've never lived here." It isn't a question.

His fingers stop moving, resting in place. "I only come to visit when Isabel's not here. She and my father are away for the weekend, hence the party to entice Mina to reengage with the real world and the masks to make it easier."

"If you didn't live here, where did you live growing up?" I ask before thinking better of it.

He tenses behind me, then slides his arm under my breasts, pressing a tender kiss to my shoulder. "Unless you plan on answering my question, I'm done sharing."

I close my eyes, wanting to tell him my real name—God, I'd give anything to hear him say it while we're in the throes of passion, but what good would it do? It's not like I'll see him again. How unfair is it that the one thing that links us together is the one night I can never discuss with him. A past I don't want but still exists. And he seems like the type who would want to know. No, he'd *have* to know. He'd never let it go.

His mother had died and he'd never lived with his father. I need to know that he had family to go home to that night he'd helped me. I'd always assumed he had. Maybe I was wrong. "I'll tell you one thing about me if you answer my question," I say quietly.

He buries his nose in my hair, inhaling deeply, then traces his fingers over my hip and up my stomach. I think he's not going to answer when he says, "I lived with my father's brother. Calder is my cousin. Uncle Jack is like a father to me."

Ah, now it makes sense. He said he'd practically grown up with Calder.

"Your turn," he says, kissing the top of my ear as his thumb leisurely slides along the inside curve of my breast.

I rest my head on his thick bicep and feel the strength of it flex under my temple. "Writing is how I express myself. Always has been. It informs, it persuades—"

"It can destroy too," he says in a clipped tone, cupping his hand on my arm. "I'm going to assume whatever transpired between you and my sister will be held in the strictest confidence."

The tension in his voice, the protectiveness reserved

for loved ones, is back. I nod. "Mina and I came to an understanding."

"Good," he says, right before he presses warm lips to my temple.

"Who's older? You or Gavin?"

"I am. Our birthdays are five months apart."

I'd studied the Blake family extensively. Isabel had Gavin ten months after she married Adam. That meant Adam hadn't had an affair while they were married, which had been my initial assumption as to why Sebastian's father hadn't acknowledged him publicly. So why *isn't* Sebastian allowed to say he's a Blake?

He slides his fingers through my hair and chuckles, an edge to his amusement. "I can practically hear the wheels turning in your investigative mind. You get one last question."

"Why won't your father acknowledge you?"

"I guess I embarrass him. A kid born to a tryst with a cocktail waitress." He shrugs and rests his chin on my shoulder. "After I first came to live with him, I was angry and rebellious. I'd just lost my mom. Isabel resented my sudden presence in their home. When I lost my birthday gift the same day my father had given it to me, Isabel accused me of hocking it for cash because 'that's what gutter trash does.' I said some not so nice things in return. Not long after, I got shipped off to live with my uncle. My father and I haven't been close since. Though I was angry at the time, moving in with my uncle was honestly the best damned thing that ever happened to me," he says, a fond smile tilting his lips.

Though his love for his uncle is obvious, I gulp, trying to clear the thickness in my throat. "What was the gift?"

He slides his hand down my arm, lacing his fingers with mine. The act melts my heart. "A watch."

I squeeze my eyes shut, holding back the mist that gathers. Guilt swells fast and furious. Before I can say anything, he rolls me over onto my back. "Tell me what makes Mina's story personal to you."

I start to shake my head, but he captures my jaw, tracing his finger along it. "I've just told you more about me than anyone else knows."

He's so sincere, I close my eyes briefly, then answer honestly. "I lost my little sister a long time ago. Forces beyond my control took her life, so I know how Mina feels losing Samantha."

He stills, his eyes searching mine. "I'm so sorry."

"Her death was so senseless. Just like Samantha's."

"Do you know why Samantha committed suicide?"

When I nod, he snorts out frustration. "That's more than we know. Mina refuses to talk about it."

I trace the worry brackets around his mouth. "Just trust that I'm going to make it right and give Mina the closure she needs."

He turns his head and presses a kiss against my palm. "I believe you. You have a way of getting what you want."

*If only that were true.* I take in the shadowed planes of his face and try to commit to memory the feel of his hard, warm body pressing close, the intoxicating smell of cologne mixed with his after-sex musk, and the arousing soreness between my legs. I ache deep inside, already mourning losing him after tonight. *I'd never let you go. Ever.*

"Did you ever get closure about your sister?" he asks, taking me by surprise. Then again, I shouldn't be. He's incredibly aware, even when he appears to be lounging, a trait of his that's both sexy and scary as hell for someone with secrets.

"Making it right for Mina will help me, yes," I say cryptically.

He holds my gaze for several seconds, and I can tell he wants to ask more, but instead he just says, "If you need my help, just ask."

I smile and drape my arms around his neck. "You've already helped me by letting me talk to Mina." *And so much more you'll never know about.*

He slides his hand down my neck to my chest, cupping my breast. Rubbing his thumb along the curve, he takes his time trailing it over my nipple. "You do realize you've just made yourself even more captivating, right? I'm ready for round two...and all the other things you're going to tell me about yourself while you're begging me to make you come," he says before he lowers his head and presses a hot kiss to my throat.

*He considers that round one? Oh shit, shit, shit!* There's no way I'll be able to keep my mouth shut if he tries to get more out of me. He's too damn good at manipulating my body. It's a wanton traitor in his hands, succumbing to his decadent sexual skills.

But even as my thoughts swirl, his lips move along my jaw, then claim mine with a heady mix of determination and predatory mastery. I'm getting caught up in the shadows we're hiding behind, things left unsaid. Sadness and regrets. I heard his when he talked about his past; I feel them in his intensity now. Tightening my arms around his neck, I kiss him, hoping to fill the void even if it's just for a little while.

Sebastian had just pulled me fully under him when the phone on his nightstand buzzes. It stops, then it buzzes again. He frowns, glancing over at the screen.

"This better be good," he grates into the phone, then he pauses and looks at me. "Yeah, I know where Scarlett is. I'll get her."

"What is it?" I ask, panic setting in. *Had Gavin figured out who I am? Did Mina tell him?*

He covers the phone. "Celeste is throwing up like a champ in the guest bathroom. Cald wants to take her home, but she's insisting on you."

"No, I'll go get her," I say, quickly sliding off the bed to grab my mask from the floor. Cass would flip if the truth came out who she really is. I hope like hell she's managed to keep her mask on.

The second I slip my mask back on, he's by my side, tilting my chin up, his voice determined. "We're not done. Nowhere near."

I can't help the fluttering in my stomach. Knowing that he wants to see me again makes me feel giddy inside even though I know it's for the best that we end it here.

"Can you meet somewhere in town tomorrow?" he asks before I can voice my anxious thoughts. "There's something I need to tell you."

I'm dying to know what that could possibly be. I really should say no, but there is one thing I need to do now, so I nod. There's a café in town with an old-fashioned covered porch. Marcus, a friend from school, told me to visit it while I was here. He said that it's perfect for enjoying coffee outside. "Do you know The Grinder? I can meet you on the porch at four in the afternoon."

He hands me my dress and corset, then traces his thumb along the edge of my mask, a victorious smile tilting his lips. "You can't hide behind this tomorrow, Red."

*I know I can't.* I dip my head, then quickly pull on my dress.

Downstairs, Calder meets us at the door, Cass

hanging on his arm. His forehead pinches in concern when she throws her arms around my neck, slurring, "Scarlett, tague me home. I feewl awfuz."

Sebastian and Calder exchange a look when the taxi I'd called drives up. "Doesn't she have a driver?" Calder asks.

*Well shit. Celeste* would *have a driver pick her up.* "Oh, she's staying with me tonight, so no driver. We decided to taxi it."

Once Cass slides across the seat, I sit down, then feel Sebastian's hand on my shoulder. "Scoot over," he says in a low tone.

I frown and shake my head. "We'll be fine, Sebastian. Go back to your party and apologize to your sister for me."

He presses his mouth in a determined slant, his hold on my shoulder tightening slightly. "I want to make sure you get home okay."

I reach up and squeeze his hand. "Really. We're good."

I jump slightly when he pushes my cape's hastily tied ribbon aside to touch the floating heart against the sensitive base of my throat. He stares at it for a second, running his finger across the gold charm, his brow furrowed as if trying to place it. I hold my breath and just as I start to pull away, he curls his fingers around mine and lifts my hand, branding a warm kiss on my palm. "Tomorrow at four."

"Tomorrow," I repeat, trying not to shiver at the sensations shimmying down my arm.

Once we've driven a couple of blocks, I instruct the cab driver to drop us off where we'd parked well away from the house. Then I pay him and half-drag, half-carry Cass to her car.

"Hmmm, you smell like cologne," she says in my ear as I hold my shoulder against her chest to keep her upright while I open the passenger's side door.

"You smell like a bar," I shoot back as she collapses into her seat.

After I've climbed in my side, I buckle her into her seat, sweat coating my face as I flop back against mine. "Honest to God, Cass. You're going to give me a heart attack," I say as I crank the engine and pull out of the parking spot.

"Who knew champagne could hit you so hard," she says, moaning slightly.

I glance her way and can't help but snicker. Her mask is pushed up into her hair and she's pressing her forehead to the cool window. "Hmm, you sound better, but you still look like shit."

"I had to play up the Celeste is a lush part before I left, but it's good to hear I look like shit, because I feel much worse than that. So glad to know I hold up well."

I smirk. "Celeste would be so proud."

My comment draws a wan smile. She turns her pale face my way. "Please tell me you at least got to talk to Mina."

I nod and turn onto a main road, my tone dry. "Yeah. And by the way, that condom popped out at the most inappropriate time."

When she giggles evilly, then winces and holds her forehead, I chuckle.

"Did you get to *use* the condom?" she asks, blinking to keep her eyes open. I guarantee it's so she won't get the spins.

"I don't kiss and tell," I say and head in the direction of her place.

"No fair. If I didn't get any, you should at least tell me about your sexcapades."

I'm a little surprised by her comment. "Didn't you hit it off with Mr. Navy?"

She nods, then frowns. "Too bad he thinks he kissed Celeste."

"Unfortunately, that's the downside of pretending to be someone you're not," I say in a low tone, knowing all too well how that truth caught me by surprise tonight. When Cass doesn't respond, I glance over to see she's already snoring lightly against the window.

# CHAPTER EIGHT

"Don't touch me! Get your hands off me!"

Panic whips me into a frenzy. I flail my arms, heart racing. Hands touch my arms in the darkness, then wrap around my shoulders, squeezing me tight. Finally, Cass's voice bleeds through. "It's a nightmare, Talia!"

I roll over onto my back, inhaling deeply through my nose, then exhaling. In and out until I feel like I'm going to faint.

Her soft hand touches my face. "You're okay. I'm right here."

I squeeze the tears back, but a few manage to escape. She brushes them away with her knuckles and then pulls me into a tight hug. "It's okay."

When I stop panting, she says, "You haven't had one of those in a while. Do you want to talk about it?"

I capture her hand and roll onto my side, pulling her with me. "No."

She snuggles close and I feel her nod against the back of my neck. "One of these days you're going to tell me."

I run my fingers across the scars on her wrist. "Just like you'll tell me, right?"

When she sighs her answer, I nod my understanding. "I love you, Cass, but you still smell like a bar."

Snickering, she hugs me close, purposefully breathing alcohol fumes across my neck. "Ugh!" I try to roll away, but she just clasps me tighter. The fact that we laugh despite our sisterly silence makes me smile even as I struggle to free myself.

"Think about the fact you finally got laid last night instead. Hold on to the positive thoughts."

Her comment makes me go still in her arms. "How did you know that?"

"Because you smell like cologne and taste like sweat." Licking my cheek, she giggles when I gag and swat her away. "And because you wouldn't tell me. That's how I know."

I don't say anything more, but as we lay there quietly the remnants of the dream linger, and my mind gets unwillingly drawn back to the first time Hayes attacked me.

Walt had just left our apartment to run an errand. I don't pay much attention to what he says, because I'm studying for a math test while I can. Amelia will be getting up from her nap in an hour.

I hear the TV blaring in the apartment next door and Hayes and Jimmy cheering for their favorite teams. I don't remember when Walt installed the door that joins our apartments, but I wish he had made it soundproof when Hayes yells through it for me to bring him a beer from our fridge. Grinding my teeth, I quickly put down my pencil and do as he asks, because I don't want Amelia to wake up early.

Jimmy shoves his shoulder-length blond hair back and winks at me as he grabs his beer from my hand.

I resist the urge to roll my eyes. He's lanky and harmless, but also around thirty-five. Yuck!

I never have liked Hayes though. Around forty, he's thin and wiry, with spiked brown hair and a ruddy complexion. The few instances I've brought them a beer or pizza that'd been delivered to our door, his dark eyes watched me with a predatory gleam as he sat there in the leather arm chair, rubbing his right ankle crossed over his left knee. I always kept my distance, and even now I stay as far back as I can and hold the beer can out for him, saying impatiently, "Here."

But he doesn't just grab the beer. He grabs my hand around it too, yanking me into his lap. The armchair swivels with my thrashing as he wraps his arms tight around my waist and laughs.

"Damn, you remind me of my old lady before she got preggo and fat," he rumbles. "That crazy bat went downhill after she whelped out my scrawny excuse for a son."

When he slides his hand up my shirt, I squeal my outrage and kick at the floor, trying to push off him and free myself. "Let me go! Walt's going to kill you!"

Jimmy's chuckling, his eyes are glassy as he watches and takes a sip of his beer.

"He won't do jack shit," Hayes says, then clamps a hand on my breast at the same time he fists his other hand in my hair. "All this long, fiery hair is such a cock-tease. Just like Brenna's used to be."

Bile gags my throat as he leans in and sniffs, grinding something hard against my butt. Is that his...oh, God! I kick his shin with the back of my foot, then his ankle at the same time I scratch his arm. Anything to get away from him.

"Fucking bitch!" He yells and yanks my hair hard, making me cry out. "Hold still, you little tease. I just want a taste."

Tears explode from my eyes, and I scream as he unsnaps my bra and grabs my breast with rough fingers. *This isn't happening. This isn't happening.*

Walt bursts through the door, his normally impassive

face a mask of fury as he quickly yanks me from Hayes' grasp. "What the fuck, Hayes! She's just a kid."

Hayes readjusts himself in his pants, then grabs up his fallen beer from the carpet. Popping it open, he shrugs as he wipes the foam on his jeans. "She got me hot, standing there all defiant-like."

Shoving me through the doorway into our apartment, Walt murmurs, "Go get Amelia...and never come in here again. Ever."

Amelia's crying for her bottle. I stumble while trying to re-hook my bra before I get to her room.

"She's fucking twelve-years-old, you perverted son of a bitch," Walt yells.

"Watch it. Don't forget who owns you," Hayes snaps back, his tone menacing.

Grabbing up Amelia's tense body, I carry her to my room and hold her close, crooning to comfort her. I quake all over as I stare out my window. My gaze locks on the fire escape and I breathe deeply, willing it to comfort me like it has in the past. When my heart continues to pound, my attention slides to the ladder. Hayes and Walt's voices have lowered, but I can still hear them. The door must not have latched when I left.

"I'm not kidding, Hayes. Keep your goddamned hands to yourself."

"Then you'd better find another way to be useful to me, because right now she's your best asset."

"I've got some ideas how to expand."

"Ideas don't mean shit, Walt. We can't expand without money. I've got a lead on a cash transaction. Some punk needs to be taken out."

"We don't kill people," Walt hisses.

Hayes snorts. "We do what needs to be done to survive, asshole. Now shut-up and watch the game."

"Stop thinking about it," Cass speaks right next to my ear, rescuing me from reliving the horrible memory on a continual loop.

I haven't dreamed about that slimy bastard Hayes in a while. I guess my talk with Mina brought all those awful memories back. I lived in fear he would walk through that door and come after me while I slept. Every night after that, when I went to bed, I shoved a chair under the door handle, not trusting the puny lock would keep him out.

I sigh and blink in the darkness. "I'm not."

"I can tell you are, because you're still tense. Why don't you tell me what happens this afternoon at four instead?"

I blink at the clock. Four a.m. I have to get up in a couple hours. "You heard that?"

She snorts. "I was drunk, not deaf."

"Just coffee," I say, relaxing as I think of Sebastian.

"Good," she says, burying her nose against the back of my neck. "And I love you too, Talia."

# CHAPTER NINE

*I* roll my shoulders in frustration as I wait in traffic heading back to the Hamptons from my aunt's place in Manhattan. I'd gotten up super early, but now I'm stuck in this never-ending line of cars.

I glance at the clock and curl my fingers tight around the steering wheel. It's almost two. At the snail's pace this traffic's flowing, I'm not sure if I'll make it to the café by four.

Sitting here gives me too much time to think. To second-guess why I'm even showing up in the first place. But my mind wars with my heart. Now that I know I possibly had a connection to the drug dealers affiliated with the group who'd blackmailed Mina—even if it was eight years ago—I really don't want Sebastian to know about my past. And that would include my real name. Why am I meeting him again?

*Because he's a good guy. You know it in your heart, Talia. It has nothing to do with the fact that you throb when you think of him, or that his name came out like a curse when you peed for the first time this morning, or that you wince whenever you move in this damned seat.*

Thoughts of Sebastian's hands roaming across my skin, their masterful play over my most intimate parts while he continued to seduce my mind, make my body heat all over again. I can't get his intensity in everything he does out of my head. From his confidence in seduction to his knowing touch, he's unforgettable, but it's the memory of his mouth crashing into mine right after he'd tied me to his bed that continues to replay over and over in my mind. Even crouched over me, with his control briefly slipping, Sebastian's kiss had been all-consuming, engaging all my senses.

Taken by surprise, a man like Sebastian doesn't allow room for other thoughts to creep in. But at his best, when he's in full control, he obliterates them completely. The moment he reined in his own desire, he orchestrated every response, directing my body to play to his tune. At that point, he became the center of my everything.

In the evening's shadows, his powerful charisma is irresistibly seductive, but in the light of day, I can't help but wonder if his formidable magnetism will be more than I can handle. I grip the steering wheel and squirm in my seat, anticipating seeing him with equal parts excitement and trepidation.

A couple hours later, I park a few stores down from The Grinder, then skirt my way behind the storefronts. Marcus had told me that the porch wraps around two sides, since the café sits on the corner at the end of the shopping strip. I decide to approach from the other side and catch a look at Sebastian in the light of day. I'm sure he's already waiting; he struck me as the type of guy who'd never be late.

The small white box in my hand crushes slightly when I spy Marcus's blond head bent over his laptop as he lounges on a leather sofa inside the café, his back against the bank of windows lining this side of the porch. What the hell is he doing here? He'd told me he was going to Florida for Spring Break. Guess those plans fell through.

I press my back against the wood-planked wall and glance up at the roof above my head. I can't believe this. Marcus will call my name out as soon as he sees me enter the cafe. And I can't guarantee he won't come outside while we're here. As my heart rate starts to ramp, it hits me; he won't recognize me with blonde hair, especially if I have my sunglasses on. Ugh...which are sitting in my car.

Before I sneak back to my car to get them, I can't help

but take a peek around the corner at Sebastian. My whole body clenches at the sight of him. He really is a brutally beautiful man. Hands tucked in his suit pockets, he's standing in front of the porch rail, watching the road intently. If I thought Gavin was intimidating in a custom made suit, Sebastian puts him to shame. He could've just as easily played the role of the wolf last night. His charcoal suit fits his broad shoulders and trim waist perfectly, obviously tailored just for his well-built physique. My gaze is drawn to his hands tucked in his pockets. Sunlight reflects off the silver of an understated cufflink standing out against his crisp white shirt.

He looks relaxed, yet his gaze never stops moving, assessing. Even though he looks the part of a billionaire, there's an underlying rawness about him that belies his cultured appearance, a don't-fuck-with-me-and-expect-to-live primal vibe. I stay back and remain still, so I don't accidentally move into his peripheral vision; the man's highly perceptive of his surroundings.

Suddenly I feel very underdressed in black slacks and a soft fitted emerald green sweater. The color would look so much better with my original color hair, but there's nothing to be done about it now. I bite my lip when my gaze lands on his blood red tie. *Had he worn it for me?* The thought makes my insides tighten.

His phone rings, drawing me out of my sexy thoughts of tugging that silk tie off and sliding my hand across his starched shirt to feel the hard planes of his chest underneath.

"Quinn." A pause, then his forehead creases. "Our orders were for Tuesday." A deep voice rumbles from his phone, but it's garbled from this distance away. Sebastian nods curtly. "Got it, sir. I'll let Blake know. We'll be there at fourteen hundred on Monday."

My eyes widen as his deferential tone and comments sink in. So his last name is Quinn. Sebastian Quinn, but which Blake is he talking about? Oh shit, is he talking about Calder? If he is, that means Sebastian's in the Navy too. Why didn't he tell me? *Why the hell do you think, idiot? He wanted to get laid. But then why bother to meet me at all?* I have no clue. It doesn't change the fact he's leaving. Just like all the men in my life have. Not that any of them have been worth a damn. I don't count my new step-uncle, George. I hardly know the man, since my aunt married him while I've been in college. But Sebastian is different. A sharp pain stabs at my chest.

His phone rings right after he clicks off with whomever he'd been speaking with. Chuckling, he puts the phone back to his ear. "Hey, talk about timing. I was just getting ready to call you—what? God!" He slides a hand through his close-cropped hair, his whole body tensing. "I'll meet you at the hospital. Hey Cald—" His voice drops to a reassuring tone. "He's going to be okay."

Sebastian stands there for a second, staring at the

road, the phone clenched in his hand, then he walks inside the café with brisk steps.

I peek through the window, watching him speak to the pony-tailed teen who approaches him with a menu and a bright smile as she looks him up and down appreciatively. He shakes his head when she gestures to an empty table, then raises his hand, palm down, as if measuring someone's height—mine. The girl shakes her head and gives him the pad and pen from her tiny apron pocket. He writes something down, then hands the paper to her.

I watch him drive away in a silver sports car, worry for whoever is on their way to the hospital tugging on my conscience, even as my heart aches. For us. For poor timing. And for my shitty past.

I know it happened like this for a reason. I don't go inside and get his contact information. It's best if I don't know it.

Sitting in my car, I scrounge up a piece of paper from my glove compartment, then write out a note. The pen dies when I decide to add something to the end. Grumbling, I toss the black pen, then dig in my purse for another and finish the note with the only pen I can find, a green one. "Super classy, Talia," I mutter. Once I finish the note, I tuck it inside the white box, then start my car and drive straight to the Blake estate.

I don't know if Mina's home. All I can do is try.

Thankfully her brothers aren't around, but when the butler tries to rebuff me from seeing Mina, I tell him, "Please tell her Scarlett is here to see her."

Mina squeals happily when she sees me at the door. Stepping out, she hugs me, her long hair flying in the wind. "I'm so happy to see you. Sebastian said you had to leave early last night." She tugs on my arm. "Come in and let's chat."

"I can't stay, Mina," I say, glad I have my dark sunglasses on so she can't see the tears misting my eyes. "I just brought this by for Sebastian. Will you please see that he gets it?"

"Of course." She wraps her fingers around the box, then gives me a secret smile. "I'll be watching the school paper."

I smile and nod. "I don't know how long it'll take to get the story published, but I'll make it happen as soon as I possibly can. And, Mina, please remember your promise to never tell anyone my name."

Confusion filters in her expression. "Not even Sebastian?"

"Not even him."

"So I should tell him this is from Scarlett?" she asks, lifting the box up.

When I nod, she tucks it under her arm. "Um, just so you know it might be a while before Sebastian gets this."

I try to keep the disappointment from my expression. "I understand."

"I don't know if he'll come back here before he leaves. He's being deployed again soon for..." She pauses, then sighs sadly, shrugging. "Who knows how long? The last time his SEAL team was gone for nine months."

"SEAL team?" I can't help the hitch in my voice.

"Yeah, he and Calder are on the same one. He didn't tell you he's a SEAL?"

I slowly shake my head. Only someone as dominant in bed as Sebastian would downplay his "lethal killing machine" status to a simple "I'm in security" statement. "I had no idea."

She nods, pride in her eyes. "But don't worry. I'll give this to him when he returns." Tapping the box's side, curiosity filters across her face. "What is it?"

I stare at the plain white box, then lift my gaze to hers. "A rainbow."

\* \* \*

Thank you for reading **MISTER BLACK! SCARLETT RED (IN THE SHADOWS, Book 2) is NOW AVAILABLE!** *Note:* *MISTER BLACK is the only novella. All the other books in the* **IN THE SHADOWS** *series are novel length.*

## SCARLETT RED

Mister Black swept in and out of my life like a tornado, leaving me twisted up and forever changed in his wake.

And now that my life is finally back on track, I need to move on, despite the many reminders of our time together.

But our pasts are only as far away as the shadows we hide behind, and sometimes those shadows grow darker, converging on the present in the most insidious way.

He is Black: a stealthy hunter and rainbow master.

I am Red: a truth seeker and desire keeper.

Together we are obsession. Passionate colors destined to be drawn together.

If you found **MISTER BLACK** an entertaining and enjoyable read, I hope you'll consider taking the time to leave a review and share your thoughts in the online bookstore where you purchased it. Your review could be the one to help another reader decide to read **MISTER BLACK** and the other books in the **IN THE SHADOWS** series! While you're on the store, grab

**SCARLETT RED** to continue with Sebastian and Talia's epic love story!

Flip the page to read an excerpt from **SCARLETT RED**!

Did you know there are **audiobooks** for the **IN THE SHADOWS** series? The audiobooks bring these stories to a whole new level. You can listen to samples and check them out on Audible and iTunes.

To KEEP up-to-date when the next P.T. Michelle book will release, join my free newsletter http://bit.ly/11tqAQN . An email will come straight to your inbox on the day a new book releases.

Why have I let this man get under my skin? Maybe he should feel some of that itchy burn. "You want to know why I took that vodka shot instead of kissing you? Because *there wasn't anything there*. No spark."

He barks out a laugh. "Does the truth *ever* come out of your mouth?" Crossing his arms, he adopts a confident stance, perfect biceps and corded muscles flexing underneath his heather gray T-shirt. "I know chemistry, and you and I, we've fucking got it in spades, sweetheart. Once you're ready to admit I'm right about *that* too, know this...." His brilliant gaze slices into me. "When I kiss you, I'll *own* you, and you'll be the one pulling my clothes off."

"Arrogant ass!" I snort. "Do you even *own* a razor?" I don't care that my dig sounds as pretentious as he accused me of being a second ago. The guy has just pushed one too many buttons. Ignoring his chuckle, I start to turn the door handle when he switches to an autocratic tone.

"Don't leave here again without me."

This is about more than my safety. I look back at him, feminine hackles raised. "You're *not* my keeper."

He lowers his arms to his sides. "Have you ever been kept? Really kept?" he asks, his voice quietly intense. "The way a woman like you should be?"

Something in his tone hits me hard and my bones start to melt at a traitorously embarrassing pace. I straighten my spine and speak past the sudden scratch in my voice. "No self-respecting woman would ever let herself be *kept*."

"So you haven't." The pleased purr in his statement, followed by a lion-like curl of his lip kindles the tiny fires flickering through me into a raging blaze.

When he takes a step forward, I cinch my hand tight on the door handle, ready to bolt, but his mesmerizing voice holds me captive. "It has everything to do with giving yourself over in a complete physical sense. I can show you exactly what that feels like." His focus travels from my face, down my body and back, leaving a singeing path in its wake. "And you'll love every aching minute of it."

**One-Click SCARLETT RED now!**

OTHER BOOKS BY P.T. MICHELLE

## In the Shadows
## (Contemporary Romance, 18+)

Mister Black (Book 1 - Talia & Sebastian, Part 1)

Scarlett Red (Book 2 - Talia & Sebastian, Part 2)

Blackest Red (Book 3 - Talia & Sebastian, Part 3)

Gold Shimmer (Book 4 - Cass & Calder, Part 1)

Steel Rush (Book 5 - Cass & Calder, Part 2)

Black Platinum (Book 6 - Talia & Sebastian, Stand Alone
Novel)

Reddest Black (Book 7 - Talia & Sebastian, Stand Alone
Novel)

Blood Rose (Book 8 - Cass & Calder, Stand Alone Novel)

Noble Brit (Book 9 - Mina & Den, Stand Alone Novel -
Coming March 2019)

## Brightest Kind of Darkness Series
## (YA/New Adult Paranormal Romance, 16+)

Ethan (Prequel)

Brightest Kind of Darkness (Book 1)

Lucid (Book 2)

Destiny (Book 3)
Desire (Book 4)
Awaken (Book 5)

## Other works by P.T. Michelle writing as Patrice Michelle

### Bad in Boots series
### (Contemporary Romance, 18+)

Harm's Hunger
Ty's Temptation
Colt's Choice
Josh's Justice

### Kendrian Vampires series
### (Paranormal Romance, 18+)

A Taste for Passion
A Taste for Revenge
A Taste for Control

## Stay up-to-date on her latest releases:

### Join P.T's Newsletter:
http://bit.ly/11tqAQN

### Visit P.T. :
**Website:** http://www.ptmichelle.com

**Twitter:** https://twitter.com/PT_Michelle
**Facebook:** https://www.
facebook.com/PTMichelleAuthor
**Instagram:** http://instagram.com/p.t.michelle
**Goodreads:** http://www.goodreads.com/author/
show/4862274.P_T_Michelle

**P.T. Michelle's Facebook Readers' Group:**
https://www.facebook.com/
groups/PTMichelleReadersGroup/

# ACKNOWLEDGMENTS

To my awesome beta readers: Joey Berube, Amy Bensette, and Magen Chambers, thank you so much for reading *MISTER BLACK* and giving honest and wonderfully helpful feedback. I'm so glad you enjoyed the smexy! You all have helped make *MISTER BLACK* an even better story.

To my fabulous critique partners, Trisha Wolfe, Rhyannon Byrd, and Julia Templeton, thank you for reading *Mister Black* and for providing your invaluable critiques. This book wouldn't be near as polished without you.

To my family, thank you for understanding the time and effort each book takes. I love you all for your wonderful support.

To my fantastic fans, thank you for loving my books and for spreading the word about them whenever you get a chance. I appreciate all your support so much!

# ABOUT THE AUTHOR

P.T. Michelle is the *NEW YORK TIMES, USA TODAY,* and International bestselling author of the contemporary romance series IN THE SHADOWS, the YA/New Adult crossover series BRIGHTEST KIND OF DARK-NESS, and the romance series: BAD IN BOOTS, KENDRIAN VAMPIRES and SCIONS (listed under Patrice Michelle). She keeps a spiral notepad with her at all times, even on her nightstand. When P.T. isn't writing, she can usually be found reading or taking pictures of landscapes, sunsets and anything beautiful or odd in nature.

To keep up-to-date when the next P.T. Michelle book will release, join P.T.'s free newsletter http://bit.ly/11tqAQN

www.ptmichelle.com

Made in United States
Troutdale, OR
10/17/2023

13792415R00094